Cathy Williams

THE SURPRISE
DE ANGELIS BABY

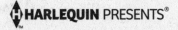

HARLEQUIN PRESENTS®

If you purchased this book without a cover you should be aware that this book is stolen property. It was reported as "unsold and destroyed" to the publisher, and neither the author nor the publisher has received any payment for this "stripped book."

Recycling programs
for this product may
not exist in your area.

ISBN-13: 978-0-373-13410-6

The Surprise De Angelis Baby

First North American Publication 2016

Copyright © 2016 by Cathy Williams

All rights reserved. Except for use in any review, the reproduction or utilization of this work in whole or in part in any form by any electronic, mechanical or other means, now known or hereinafter invented, including xerography, photocopying and recording, or in any information storage or retrieval system, is forbidden without the written permission of the publisher, Harlequin Enterprises Limited, 225 Duncan Mill Road, Don Mills, Ontario M3B 3K9, Canada.

This is a work of fiction. Names, characters, places and incidents are either the product of the author's imagination or are used fictitiously, and any resemblance to actual persons, living or dead, business establishments, events or locales is entirely coincidental.

This edition published by arrangement with Harlequin Books S.A.

For questions and comments about the quality of this book, please contact us at CustomerService@Harlequin.com.

® and TM are trademarks of Harlequin Enterprises Limited or its corporate affiliates. Trademarks indicated with ® are registered in the United States Patent and Trademark Office, the Canadian Intellectual Property Office and in other countries.

HARLEQUIN®
www.Harlequin.com

Printed in U.S.A.

Cathy Williams can remember reading Harlequin Presents books as a teenager, and now that she is writing them she remains an avid fan. For her, there is nothing like creating romantic stories and engaging plots, and each and every book is a new adventure. Cathy lives in London, and her three daughters—Charlotte, Olivia and Emma—have always been, and continue to be, the greatest inspirations in her life.

Books by Cathy Williams

Harlequin Presents

The Wedding Night Debt
A Pawn in the Playboy's Game
At Her Boss's Pleasure
The Real Romero
The Uncompromising Italian
The Argentinian's Demand
Secrets of a Ruthless Tycoon
Enthralled by Moretti
His Temporary Mistress
A Deal with Di Capua
The Secret Casella Baby
The Notorious Gabriel Diaz
A Tempestuous Temptation

The Italian Titans

Wearing the De Angelis Ring

One Night With Consequences

Bound by the Billionaire's Baby

Seven Sexy Sins

To Sin with the Tycoon

Protecting His Legacy

The Secret Sinclair

Visit the Author Profile page at Harlequin.com for more titles.

CHAPTER ONE

COULD THE DAY get any better?

Daniel De Angelis stepped out from the air-conditioned comfort of his black chauffeur-driven Mercedes and removed his dark sunglasses to scan the scenery around him.

Frankly—perfect. Brilliant sunshine glinted on the calm turquoise water of the Aegean Sea. He'd never made it to Santorini before, and he took a few minutes to appreciate the scenic view of the bowl-shaped harbour from where he stood, looking down on it from a distance. He could even make out the vessel he had come to snap up at a bargain price.

It looked as picture-perfect as everything around it, but that, of course, was an illusion. It was semi-bankrupt, on its last legs—a medium-sized cruise ship which he would add to his already vast portfolio of conquests.

He knew down to the last detail how much money it had lost in the past five years, how much it owed the bank, how much its employees were paid, how discounted their fares were now they were desperate to get customers… He practically knew what the owners had for their breakfast and where they did their food shopping.

As with all deals, big or small, it always paid to do his homework. His brother, Theo, might have laughingly referred to this extravagant purchase as nothing more than a toy—something different to occupy him for a few months—but it was going to be a relatively expensive toy, and he intended to use every trick in the book to make sure he got the best possible deal.

Thinking about his brother brought a grin to his face. Who'd have thought it? Who would have thought that Theo De Angelis would one day be singing the praises of the institution of marriage and waxing lyrical about the joys of love? If he hadn't heard it with his own ears when he had spoken to his brother earlier in the week then *he* wouldn't have believed it.

He looked around him with the shrewd eyes of a man who knew how to make money and wondered what he could do here. Exquisite scenery. Exquisite island, if you could somehow get rid of the hordes of annoying tourists milling around everywhere. Maybe in the future he would think about exploiting this little slice of paradise, but for the moment there was an interesting acquisition at hand, and one which would have the benefit of his very personal input—which was something of a rarity. He was relishing this break from the norm.

Then there was his successful ditching of the last woman he had been dating, who had become a little too clingy for comfort.

And, last but not least on the feel-good spectrum, a sexy little blonde thing would be waiting for him when his time was up on that floating liner so far from paradise…

All in all this was going to be something of a holiday and, bearing in mind the fact that he hadn't had one of those in the longest while, Daniel was in high spirits.

'Sir? Maybe we should head down so that you can board the ship? It's due to leave soon…'

'Shame… I've only been here for a few hours.' Daniel turned to his driver, whom he had brought with him from the other side of the world on an all-expenses-paid, fun in the sun holiday, with only a spot of driving to do here and there. 'I feel Santorini could be just the place for me... Nice exclusive hotel somewhere... Kick back and relax...'

'I didn't think you knew how to do that, sir.'

Daniel laughed. Along with his brother and his father, Antonio Delgado was one of only a few people in whom he had absolute trust, and in fairness his driver probably knew more about his private life than both his brother *and* his father, considering he drove him to his numerous assignations with numerous women and had been doing so for the past decade.

'You're right.' He briskly pulled open the car door and slid inside, appreciating the immediate drop in temperature. 'Nice thought, though...'

In truth, kicking back by the side of a pool with a margarita in one hand and a book in the other wasn't his thing.

He kicked back in the gym occasionally, on the slopes occasionally and far more frequently in bed—and his women all ran to type. Small, blonde, sexy and very, very obliging.

Granted, none of them stayed the course for very long, but he saw that as just an occupational hazard for a man whose primary focus—like his brother's—had always been on work. He thrived on the pressure of a high-octane, fast-paced work-life filled with risk.

He had benefited from the privileges of a wealthy background, but at the age of eighteen, just as he had done with Theo, his father, Stefano De Angelis, had told him that his fortune was his to build or not to build as the case might be. Family money would kick-start his career up to a certain point, but that would be it. He would fly or fall.

And, like Theo, he had flown.

Literally. To the other side of the world, where he had taken the leisure industry by storm, starting small and getting bigger and bigger so that now, at not yet thirty, he owned hotels, casinos and restaurants across Australia and the Far East.

He had acquired so much money that he could spend the remainder of his life taking time out—next to that pool with a book in one hand and a margarita in the other—and *still* live in the sort of style that most people could only ever dream of. But work was his passion and he liked it that way.

And this particular acquisition was going to be novel and interesting.

'Don't forget,' he reminded Antonio, 'you're to drop me off fifteen minutes away from the port.'

'It's boiling out there, sir. Are you sure you wouldn't rather enjoy the air-conditioning in the car for as long as possible?'

'A little discomfort won't kill me, Antonio, but I'm deeply touched by your concern.' He caught his driver's eye in the rearview mirror and grinned. 'No, it's essential that I hit the cruise ship like any other passenger. Arriving in the back seat of a chauffeur-driven Merc isn't part of the plan.'

The plan was to check out the small cruise liner incognito. The thing hadn't made a buck in years, and he wanted to see for himself exactly where the myriad problems lay. Mismanagement, he was thinking. Lazy staff, incompetence on every level...

He would spend a few days checking out the situation and making a note of who he would sack and who he would consider taking on as part of his team when the liner was up and running in its new format.

Judging from the list of airy-fairy scheduled activities, he was thinking that the entire lot would be destined for unemployment.

Five days. That was the time scale he had in mind, at the end of which he would stage his takeover. He didn't anticipate any problems, and he had big plans for the liner. Forget about woolly lectures and cultural visits while on board substandard food was served to passengers who frankly wouldn't expect much more, considering the pittance they were paying for their trips.

He intended to turn the liner into one of unparalleled luxury, for a wealthy elite whose every whim would be indulged as they were ferried from golf course to golf course in some of the most desirable locations in the world. He would decide on the destinations once the purchase was signed, sealed and delivered.

As with every other deal he had successfully completed, Daniel had utter confidence that he would succeed with this one and that the ship would prove to be a valuable asset. He had never failed and he had no reason to assume that this would prove the exception.

At the port, with the shiny black Merc behind him and a battered backpack bought especially for the purpose slung over his shoulder, he cast a jaundiced eye over the motley crew heading onto the liner.

Already he could see that the thing was in a deplorable state. How could Gerry Ockley, who had inherited this potential goldmine from his extremely wealthy father, have managed so thoroughly to turn it into something that no self-respecting pirate would have even considered jumping aboard to plunder? How the hell could he ever have imagined that some wacky cultural cruise would actually turn a profit?

True, it had taken over eight years to run it into the ground, but he would have thought that someone—bank manager…good friend…concerned acquaintance…*wife*— would have pointed him in the right direction at some point.

The liner was equipped to hold two hundred and fifty passengers comfortably, in addition to all the crew

needed. Daniel figured that at present it was half full—
if that.

He would be joining it halfway through its trip and,
ticket at the ready, he joined the chattering groups of
people, mostly in their mid-fifties and early sixties, who
were gathering in preparation for boarding.

Did he blend in? No. When it came to anyone under
the age of thirty-five, as far as he could tell he was in the
minority. And at six foot two he was taller than nearly
everyone else there.

But he was in no doubt that he would be able to fend
off any curious questions, and he was tickled pink that he
would be travelling incognito for the next few days. Was
that really necessary? Possibly not. He could always have
stayed where he was, in his plush offices in Australia, and
formulated a hostile takeover. But this, he thought, would
afford him the opportunity of removing at least some of
the hostility from his takeover.

He would be able to tell Ockley and his wife exactly
why he was taking over and exactly *why* they couldn't refuse him. He would be able to point out all the significant
shortcomings of their business and he would be able to
do that from the advantageous perspective of someone
who had been on board their liner. He was being kind,
and in the process would enjoy the experience. The fact
that the experience would be reflected in his offer would
be a nice bonus.

He could feel inquisitive eyes on him as the crowd of
people narrowed into something resembling an orderly
queue. With the ease born of habit he ignored them all.

His appearance matched his battered backpack. He was
just a broke traveller on a cut-price cultural tour of the
Greek islands and possibly Italy. His hair, a few shades
lighter than his brother's, was slightly longer than he normally wore it, curling at the nape of his neck, and as he

hadn't shaved that morning his face was shadowed with bristle. His eyes, however, the same unusual shade of green as his brother's, were shrewd as they skimmed the crowds. He had tucked his sunglasses into his pocket.

The sun was ferocious. He could feel himself perspiring freely under the faded polo shirt and realised he shouldn't have worn jeans. Fortunately, he had a few pairs of khaki shorts in the backpack, along with an assortment of tee shirts, and those should do the trick in the blistering sun once he was on board the liner.

He switched off the thought, his mind already moving to work, planning how he would co-ordinate the work to be done on the liner and the time when it would be ready to set sail in its new, improved condition. He would charge outrageous prices for anyone lucky enough to secure a ticket, and he had no doubt that people would be queuing to pay.

Done deal.

He hadn't felt this relaxed in ages.

Delilah Scott eyed her mobile, which was buzzing furiously at her, and debated whether she should pick it up or not.

Her sister's name was flashing on the screen, demanding urgent attention.

With a little sigh of resignation she answered, and was greeted with a flurry of anxious questions.

'Where on earth have you been? I've been trying to get through to you for the past two days! You know how I worry, Delly! It's mad here, with the shop... I can't believe you've decided, just like that, to extend your holiday! You *know* I'm depending on you getting back here to help... I can't do it on my own...'

Delilah felt her stomach churn into instant nervous knots.

'I—I know, Sarah,' she stammered, gazing through the tiny porthole of her very small cabin, which was just big enough for a single bed, the very barest of furniture, and an absolutely minuscule en-suite shower room. 'But I thought the added experience would come in handy for when I get back to the Cotswolds… It's not like I'm on *holiday*…' she tacked on guiltily.

'You *are* on holiday, Delly!' her sister said accusingly. 'When you said that you'd be doing some teaching for a fortnight, I never expected you to send me an email telling me that you'd decided to extend the fortnight into *six weeks*! I *know* you really needed to get away, Delly…what with that business with Michael…but *still*… It's *manic* here…'

Delilah felt the worry pouring down the phone line and experienced another wave of guilt.

Back home, Sarah was waiting for her. Building work which was costing an absolute arm and a leg was set to begin in two weeks' time, and she knew that her sister had been waiting for her to get back so that they could weather it together.

But was it too much to take a bit of time off before the dreadful drudgery of normal life returned? She had just completed her art degree, and every single free moment during those three years she had been in that tiny cottage with her sister, worrying about how they were going to survive and counting the takings from the gallery downstairs in the certain knowledge that sooner or later Dave Evans from the bank was going to lose patience and foreclose.

And then there had been Michael…

She hated thinking about him—hated the way just remembering how she had fallen for him, how he had messed her around, made her feel sick and foolish at the same time.

She definitely didn't want to hear Sarah rehashing that horrible catastrophe. Delilah loved her sister, but ever since she could remember Sarah had mothered her, had made decisions for her, had worried on her behalf about anything and everything. The business with Michael had just fed into all that concern. Yes, it was always great to have the comfort of someone's love and empathy when you'd just had your heart broken, but it could also be claustrophobic.

Sarah cared so much…always had…

Their parents, Neptune and Moon, both gloriously irresponsible hippies who had been utterly and completely wrapped up in one another, had had little time to spare for their offspring. Both artists, they had scratched a living selling some of their art, and later on a random assortment of crystals and gems after their mother had become interested in alternative healing.

They had converted their cottage into a little gallery and had just about managed to survive because it was slap-bang in the middle of tourist territory. They had always benefited from that. But when they had died—within months of one another, five years previously—sales of local art had already begun to take a nosedive and things had not improved since.

Sarah, five years older than Delilah, had been doing the best she could, making ends meet by doing the books for various people in the small village where they lived, but it had always been understood that once Delilah had completed her art degree she would return and help out.

As things stood, they had taken out a substantial loan to fund renovations to the gallery, in order to create a new space at the back where Delilah would teach art to anyone local who was interested and, more importantly, other people, keen on learning to draw and paint, who would perhaps attend week-long courses, combining sightseeing in the picturesque Cotswolds with painting indoors and outdoors.

It was all a brilliant if last-ditch idea, and whilst Delilah had been totally in favour of it she had suddenly, when offered the opportunity to extend her stay on board the *Rambling Rose*, been desperate to escape.

A little more time to escape the finality of returning to the Cotswolds and to breathe a little after her breakup from Michael.

Just a little more time to feel normal and relaxed.

'It'll be brilliant experience for when I get back,' she offered weakly. 'And I've transferred most of my earnings to the account. I'll admit I'm not on a fabulous amount, but I'm making loads of good contacts here. Some of the people are really interested in the courses we'll be offering...'

'Really?'

'Honestly, Sarah. In fact, several have promised that they'll be emailing you for details about prices and stuff in the next week or so.'

'Adrian's just about finished doing the website. That's more money we're having to expend...'

Delilah listened and wondered whether these few weeks on the liner were to be her only window of freedom from worrying. Sarah would not countenance selling the cottage and Delilah, in fairness, would have hated to leave her family home. But staying required so many sacrifices that she felt as though her youth would be eaten up in the process. She was only twenty-one now, but she could see herself saying goodbye to her twenties in the never-ending task of just making ends meet.

She had had a vision of having fun, of feeling young when she had been going out with Michael, but that had been a very narrow window and in the end it had just been an idiotic illusion anyway. When she thought about him now she didn't think of *fun*, she just thought of being stupid and naïve.

She knew that she was playing truant by extending her stay here, but the responsibilities waiting for her wouldn't be going anywhere…and it was nice not being mothered by her sister, not having every move she made frowningly analysed, not having her life prescribed because Sarah knew best…

She hung up, relieved to end the conversation, and decided to spend what remained of the evening in her cabin.

Maybe she would ask a couple of the other teachers on the liner—young girls, like herself—to have something to eat with her in the cabin, maybe play cards and joke about some of the passengers, who mostly reminded her of her parents. Free-spirited ageing hippies, into all sorts of weird and wonderful arty pastimes and hobbies.

Tomorrow, she would be back to teaching, and she had a full schedule ahead of her…

Daniel stretched. Peered through the porthole to a splendid view of deep blue ocean. The night before he had enjoyed an expected below average meal—though not sitting at the captain's table. That sort of formality didn't exist aboard this liner. It seemed to be one big, chattering, happy family of roughly one hundred people, of varying ages, and fifty-odd crew members who all joined in the fun. He had mixed and circulated but he knew that he'd stuck out like a sore thumb.

Now, breakfast…and then he would begin checking out the various classes—all of which seemed destined to make no money. Pottery, poetry writing, art, cookery and a host of others, including some more outlandish ones, like astronomy and palm reading.

Today he ditched the jeans in favour of a pair of low slung khaki shorts, a faded grey polo shirt and deck shoes, which he used on his own sailing boat when he occasionally took to the sea.

He paused, in passing, to glance in the mirror.

He saw what he always saw. A lean, bronzed face, green eyes, thick dark lashes, dirty blond hair streaked from the Australian sun. When he had time for sport he preferred it to be extreme, and his body reflected that. Boxing sessions at the gym, sailing on his own for relaxation, skiing on black runs…

It was after nine, and on the spur of the moment he decided to skip breakfast, pulling a map of the liner from his pocket and, after discarding some of the more outrageous courses, heading for the section of the liner where the slightly less appalling ones were taking place.

He had no idea what to expect. Every single passenger seemed to be an enthusiastic member of some course or other, and as he made his way through the ship, his sharp eyes noting all the signs of dilapidation, he peered into full classes. Some people were on deck, enjoying the sun, but it had to be said that the majority had come for the educational aspect of the cruise.

It took all sorts, he thought as he meandered through the bowels of the liner.

Inside the ship, as outside, it was very hot. The rooms in which the various courses were being taught were all air-conditioned, and for no better reason than because his clothes were beginning to stick to him like glue, he pushed open one of the doors and stepped inside.

In the midst of explaining the technique for drawing perspective, Delilah looked up and…

Her breath caught in her throat.

Lounging indolently by the door was the most stunningly beautiful man she had ever seen in her life. He definitely hadn't joined the cruise when they had started.

He must have embarked in Santorini, a late member of the passenger list.

He was tall. *Very* tall. And built like an athlete. Even wearing the standard gear of nearly every other passenger on the liner—longish shorts and a tee shirt—it was impossible to miss the honed muscularity of his body.

'May I help you?'

Everyone had turned to stare at the new recruit and she smartly called them back to attention, and to the arrangement of various little ceramic pots they had been in the process of trying to sketch.

Daniel had been expecting many things, but he hadn't been expecting this. The girl looking at him questioningly was tall and reed-slender and her hair was a vibrant shade of copper—a thousand different shades from red through to auburn—and had been tugged back into a loose ponytail which hung over one shoulder.

He sauntered into the room and looked around him at the twenty or so people, all seated in front of canvasses. A long shelf at the back held various artists' materials and on the walls several paintings were hanging—presumably efforts from the members of the class.

'If I'm interrupting I can always return later…'

'Not at all, Mr…?'

'Daniel.' He held out his hand and the girl hurried forward and briefly shook it. 'I joined the cruise yesterday,' he expanded, 'and I haven't had time to sign up to any of the courses…'

'But you're interested in art?' That brief meeting of hands had sent a sharp little frisson skittering through her and it was all she could do to maintain eye contact with him. 'I'm Delilah Scott, and I'm in charge of the art course…'

Up close, he was truly spectacular. With an artist's eye she could appreciate the perfect symmetry of his lean face. The brooding amazing eyes, the straight nose and the wide, sensual mouth. His hair looked sun-washed—not quite blond, but nothing as dull as brown—and there was something about him…something strangely charismatic that rescued him from being just another very good-looking guy.

She would love to paint him. But right now…

'I can explain the course that I run…'

She launched into her little set speech and edged slightly away, because standing too close was making her feel jumpy. She'd had enough of men to last a lifetime, and the last thing she needed was to start feeling jumpy around one now.

'Of course I don't know what standard you're at, but I'm sure you'll be able to fit in whether you're a complete beginner or at a more intermediary level. I can also show you my qualifications… You would have to return later to get the proper lowdown, because as you can see I'm in the middle of taking a class and this one will last until lunchtime… But perhaps you'd like to see some of the work my class have been doing…?'

Not really, Daniel thought, but he tilted his head to one side and nodded with a show of interest.

She was as graceful as a ballerina. He liked women curvy and voluptuous. This girl was anything but. She was willowy, and dressed in just the sort of appalling clothes he disliked on a woman. A loose ankle-length skirt in a confusing number of clashing colours and a floaty top that left way too much to the imagination.

Personally, he had never been a big fan of having to work on his imagination when it came to women. He liked to see what he was getting, and he'd never had any trouble in finding beautiful women keen to oblige. Small, tight clothes showing off curves in all the right places… Girls who were in it for fun, no-strings-attached relationships. True, the occasional woman might get a little too wrapped up in planning for a future that wasn't going to happen, but that was fine. He just ditched her. And not once had he ever felt a qualm of guilt or unease about doing that because he was straight with every single one of them upfront.

He wasn't ready for marriage. He wasn't even in it for anything approaching long term. He didn't want a partner to meet his family and close friends and start getting ideas. He didn't do home-cooked meals or watching telly or anything remotely domesticated.

He thought of Kelly Close and his lips thinned. Oh, no, he didn't do *any* of that stuff…

As far as Daniel De Angelis was concerned, at this point in his life work was way more important than women, and when and if he decided to tie the knot—which was nowhere in the near future, especially as Theo was now happily planning a big wedding himself, thereby paving the way for Daniel to take his time getting there—he intended to marry someone who didn't just see the benefits of his bank balance.

He'd had his brush with a scheming gold-digger and once was plenty enough. Kelly Close—an angelic vision with the corrupt heart of a born opportunist. He slammed the door on pointless introspection. Enough that she had been a valuable learning curve. Now he had fun. Uncomplicated fun with sexy little things, like the blonde who would be waiting for him when he jumped ship.

Delilah Scott was showing him around the room, encouraging him to look at what the aspiring artists had already accomplished while they had been on the cruise.

'Fascinating,' he murmured. Then he turned to her before she could conclude the tour. 'So—lunch. Where shall we meet and what time?'

'Sorry?' Delilah asked in confusion.

'You said you wanted to give me the lowdown on the course. Over lunch sounds good. When and where? I'm guessing there's only one restaurant on the liner?'

Delilah felt a rush of heat swamp her and sharply brought herself back down to earth. 'Did I say that? I didn't think I had. You're more than welcome to just turn up tomorrow morning for the class, or you could join in right now if you like... There's lots of paper...pencils...'

Those amazing green eyes, the opaque colour of burnished glass, made her want to stare and keep on staring.

'I intend to spend the morning considering my options,' Daniel inserted smoothly. 'Checking out what the other courses are...whether they're more up my street... I'll meet you for lunch at twelve-thirty in the restaurant. You can tell me all about your course and see whether it fits the bill or not...'

Not his type, but eye-catching all the same. Skin as smooth as satin, sherry-coloured eyes, and she was pale gold after time spent in the sun. And her mouth... Its full lips parted now as she looked at him.

'I don't think there's any need for me to explain the course over *lunch*...'

'You're in the service industry... Surely that implies that you have to serve the customer? I'm just after some information...'

'I know that, but...'

But Michael had left her wary of men like this one. Good-looking men who were a little offbeat, a little off the beaten track...

Eight months ago Michael Connor had sauntered into her life—all long, dark hair and navy blue eyes and a sexy, sexy smile that had blown her away. At twenty-seven, he already had a fledgling career in photography, and he had charmed her with the amazing photos he had taken over the years. He had wined and dined her and talked about taking her to the Amazon, so that she could paint and he could take pictures.

He had swept her away from all her miserable, niggling worries about money and held out a shimmering vision of adventure and excitement. Two free spirits travelling the world. She had fallen in love with him and with those thrilling possibilities. She had dared to think that she had found a soul mate—someone with whom she could spend the rest of her life. They had kissed, but he hadn't pressed her into bed, and now she wondered how long he would have bided his time until deciding that kissing and cuddling wasn't what he was in it for.

Not much longer—because he'd already had a girlfriend. Someone in one of those countries he had visited. She'd chanced upon the fact only because she had happened to see a text message flash up on his screen. When she had confronted him, he'd laughed and shrugged. So he wasn't the settling down type…? He had an open relationship with his girlfriend so what was the big deal…? He had lots of women…he was single, wasn't he? And he'd hung around with *her*, hadn't he? She hadn't *really* thought that they were going to get married and have two point two kids and a dog, had she?

She had misread him utterly. She'd been taken in by a charming facade and by her own longing for a little adventure.

She'd been a fool.

Her sister had always sung the praises of stability and a good old-fashioned guy who could provide, whose feet were firmly planted on the ground. She'd seen no virtue in their parents' chaotic lives, which had left them with debt and financial worries.

She should have paid more attention to those sermons.

'I won't occupy a lot of your time,' Daniel murmured,

intrigued by this woman who didn't jump at the offer of having a meal with him.

Delilah blinked, ready to shake her head in instant refusal.

'There's a bar… We can have something light and you can tell me all about your course. You can sell it to me.' He flung his hands wide in a gesture that was both exotic and self-deprecating at the same time. 'I'm caught on the horns of a dilemma…' Again, he found it weirdly invigorating to actually be in the position of trying to *persuade* a woman to join him for a meal 'You wouldn't want to drive a man into the arms of learning palmistry, would you?'

Delilah swallowed down a responding smile. 'I suppose if you really think it's that important…'

'Great. I'll see you in the bar at twelve-thirty. You can hone your pitch before we meet…'

Delilah watched as he strolled out of the room. She felt as though she had been tossed into a tumble drier with the speed turned to high and she didn't like it. But she'd agreed to meet him and she would keep their meeting brief and businesslike.

She could barely focus on her class for the next three hours. Her mind was zooming ahead to meeting Daniel in the bar. And sure enough when, at a little after twelve-thirty, she hesitantly walked into the small saloon bar, which was already filling up with passengers whose courses had likewise ended for the morning, there he was. Seated at a small table, nursing a drink in front of him.

He was eye-catching—and not just because he was noticeably younger than everyone else. He would have been eye-catching in any crowd. She threaded her way through to him, pausing to chat to some of the other passengers.

Daniel watched her with lazy, deceptive indolence. He hadn't boarded this third-rate liner for adventure. He had boarded it for information.

He looked at her narrowly, thoughts idly playing through his head. She seemed to know everyone and she was popular. He could tell from the way the older passengers laughed in her company, totally at ease. He was sure that she would be equally popular amongst the staff.

Who was worth keeping on? Who would get the sack immediately? He wouldn't need any of the teachers on board, but the crew would be familiar with the liner, would probably have proved themselves over a number of years and might be an asset to him. It would certainly save him having to recruit from scratch and then face the prospect of some of them not being up to the task. When it came to pleasing the wealthy there could be no room for error.

Would she be able to help him with the information he needed? Naturally he wouldn't be able to tell her why...

Not for a second did Daniel see this as any form of deception. As far as he was concerned he would merely be making the most of a possible opportunity, no harm done.

He rose as she finally approached him.

'You came,' he said with a slashing smile, indicating the chair next to him. 'I wasn't sure whether you would. You seemed a little reluctant to take me up on my offer.'

'I don't normally fraternise with the passengers,' Delilah said stiffly as she sat down.

'You seemed familiar enough with them just then...'

'Yes, but...'

'What can I get you to drink?'

His eyes roved over her colt-like frame. He watched the way her fingers nervously played with the tip of her ponytail and the way her eyes dipped to avoid his. If he had had the slightest suspicion that she knew who he was he might have wondered whether her shyness was some kind of act to stir his interest—because women, in his company, were usually anything but coy.

'Just some juice, please.' Delilah was flustered by the way he looked at her—as though he could see straight into her head.

Juice in hand, and with a refill of whisky for him, he returned to settle into the chair and looked at her.

'So, you wanted to know about the course…'

Delilah launched into chatter. She found that she was drawn to look at him, even though she didn't want to. It wasn't just that he was a passenger—something about him sent disturbing little chills racing up and down her spine and sent her alarm bells into overdrive.

'I've brought some brochures for you to have a look at…'

She rummaged in her capacious bag and extracted a few photocopied bits of paper, which she self-consciously thrust at him. Several had samples of her work printed inside, and these he inspected, glancing between her face and the paintings she had done at college.

'Impressive,' he mused.

'Have you seen any other courses that interest you? Aside…' She allowed herself a polite smile. 'Aside from the palmistry?'

'I'm tempted by astronomy… When it comes to stars, I feel I could become something of an expert…' Daniel murmured. His last girlfriend had been an actress. Did that count? 'But, no…' He sat back briskly, angling his chair so that he could stretch his legs to one side. 'I'm only here for a week. Probably just to take in a couple of stops. I think I'll go for yours…'

A week? Delilah felt an inexplicable surge of disappointment, but she pinned a smile on her face and kept it there as she sipped some of the orange juice.

'Well, I can't guarantee I can turn you into Picasso at the end of a week… I mean, most of the other passengers

are here for the full month, and then we have more joining us when we dock at Naples...'

'Seems a bit haphazard,' Daniel said. 'Put it this
way—I managed to get a place at the last minute, and
for whatever duration I chose...'

'It's...it's a little more informal than most cruises, I
guess,' Delilah conceded. 'But that's because it's a fam-
ily-run business. Gerry and Christine *like* the fact that
people can dip in and out...'

'Gerry and Christine?'

Ockley. He knew their names, knew how far into debt
they were. Little wonder people could dip in and out of
the cruise at whim. Any business was good business when
it came to making ends meet.

'They run the cruise ship. Actually, it's theirs, and
they're great.'

She felt herself relax, because he was so clearly interested in what she was saying. He was just another keen
passenger, and if his looks made her a bit jittery then that
was *her* problem and, after the debacle with Michael, it
was one she could easily deal with.

'Are they? In what way?'

'Just very interested in all the passengers—and the
crew have been with them for ages.'

'Is that a fact...? And I guess you know all the crew...?'

'They're wonderful. Devoted to their jobs. They all
love the fact that they're pretty much allowed free rein
with what they do... Of course they all follow the rules,
but for instance the chef is allowed to do as he likes and
so is the head of entertainment. I've been very lucky to
get this job...' She guiltily thought of her sister, but she
would be back home soon and all would be fine.

Daniel saw the shadow cross her face and for a few
seconds was intrigued enough to want to find out more
about the woman sitting in front of him. But there was no

time in his busy, compacted schedule for curiosity about a random stranger, however strangely attractive he might find her. He had to cut to the chase.

'So…' He carried the conversation along briskly. 'Tomorrow…what time do we start…?'

CHAPTER TWO

'Now HAVE A look at the jug. George…see how it forms the centre of the arrangement? With the other two pieces in the background? So that the whole forms a geometric shape…? If you could just make the jug a teeny bit smaller, then I think we're getting there!'

For the umpteenth time Delilah's eyes skittered towards the door, waiting for it to be pushed open by Daniel.

Her calm, peaceful enjoyment of her brief window of freedom appeared to have disappeared the moment she had met the man. She had been knocked sideways by his looks, but more than that he had a certain watchfulness about him that she found weirdly compelling…

She was seeing him through the eyes of an *artist*, she had told herself, over and over again. The arrangement of his features, the peculiar aura of authority and power he emanated was quite unlike anything she had ever seen before in anyone.

She had laughingly told herself that she was reading far too much into someone who was probably a drifter, working his way through the continent. Someone who had managed to accumulate sufficient money to buy himself a few days on the liner so that he could pursue a hobby. Most of the passengers were in their fifties or sixties, on the cruise for the whole time, but there were a number who, like him, were on the cruise for a limited period of time, taking advantage of one or other of the many courses offered while enjoying the ports before disembarking so that they could continue travelling.

He was a traveller.

But she still found herself searching out the door every two minutes, and when—an hour after the class had begun—he pushed it open and strolled into the room she drew her breath in sharply.

'Class!' Everyone instantly stopped what they were doing and looked at Daniel. 'I'd like to introduce a new recruit! His name is Daniel and he's an aspiring artist, so I hope you'll welcome him in and show him the ropes if I happen to be busy with someone. Daniel... I've set aside a seat for you, with an easel. You never mentioned what level you feel you might be at...?'

Daniel didn't think that there was *any* level that might apply to him. 'Basic.' He smiled, encompassing every single person in the room, and was met with smiles in return, before their attention reverted to their masterpieces in the making.

'In that case, why don't you start with pencil? You can choose whichever softness you feel comfortable with and perhaps try your hand at reproducing the arrangement on the table in front of the class...'

She was extremely encouraging. She had kind things to say about even the most glaringly amateurish efforts. She took time to help and answered all the questions thrown at her patiently. When he told her, as he stared at the empty paper pinned to his easel, that he was waiting for inspiration to come and that you couldn't rush that sort of thing, she didn't roar with laughter but merely suggested that a single stroke of the pencil might be all the inspiration he needed.

He thought that he might have been a little more interested in art at school if he'd had *her* as his teacher instead of the battleaxe who had told him that the world of art would be better off without his input. Not that she hadn't had a point…

He'd managed something roughly the shape of one of the objects on the table by the time the class drew to an end, but instead of heading out with everyone else he remained exactly where he was, watching as she tidied everything away.

Delilah could feel his eyes on her as she busied herself returning pencils and foam pads and palette knives to the various boxes on the shelf. She'd been so conscious of him sitting there at the back of the class, sprawled out with his body at an angle and doing absolutely nothing, from what she could see. She'd barely been able to focus.

Now she turned to him and smiled politely. 'Won't you be joining the other passengers for some lunch?' she asked as she began the process of dismounting the easels and stacking them away neatly against the wall, where straps had been rigged to secure them in place.

Daniel linked his fingers behind his head and relaxed back into the chair. 'I thought you could give me some pointers on my efforts today…' He swivelled the easel so that it was facing her and Delilah walked slowly towards it.

'I'm sorry you haven't managed to accomplish a bit more,' she said tactfully. 'I was aiming for more of a *realistic* reproduction of the jugs…it's important to really try and *replicate* what you see at this stage of your art career…'

'I don't think I'll be having a career in art,' Daniel pointed out.

'So this is just a hobby for you…? Well, that's good, as well. Hobbies can be very relaxing, and once you become a bit more familiar with the pencil—once your confidence starts growing—you'll find it the most relaxing thing in the world…'

'Is that what *you* do to relax?' he asked, making no move to shift.

'I really must get on and tidy away this stuff…'

'No afternoon classes?'

'The afternoons, generally speaking, are downtime for everyone. The passengers like to go out onto the deck, or else sit in the shade and catch up with their reading or whatever homework's been set…'

'And what do *you* do?'

'I… I do a little painting…sometimes I sit by the pool on the top deck and read…'

Daniel enjoyed the way she blushed. It was a rare occurrence. The women he dated had left their blushing days far behind.

'I thought we might have lunch again today,' he suggested, waiting to see what form her refusal would take. 'As you can see…' he waved in the vague direction of his easel '…my efforts at art are crap.'

'No one's efforts at art are anything but good. You forget that beauty is in the eye of the beholder…'

'How long are you going to be on the liner for?'

'I beg your pardon?'

'Are you here for…?' He whipped out the crumpled cruise brochure from his shorts pocket, twisted it in various directions before finding the bit he wanted. 'For the full duration of a month?'

'I can't see what this has to do with the course, Mr… er… Daniel…'

'If you're going to be on the course for the full duration I *might* be incentivised to stay a bit longer than a week.'

Complete lie—but something about her appealed to him. Yet again she was in an outfit more suitable for one of the middle-aged free spirits on the cruise ship. Another flowing skirt in random colours, and another kind of loose, baggy top that worked hard at concealing her figure—which, he saw as he surreptitiously cast his eye over it, was as slender and as graceful as a gazelle's.

The libido he had planned on resting while he was on the ship stirred into enthusiastic life as he wondered what the body under the unappealing clothes might be like.

He went for big breasts. She was flat-chested—that much he could see. He went for women who were small and curvy—she was long and willowy. He liked them blonde and blue-eyed. She was copper-haired and brown-eyed.

Maybe it was the novelty... But whatever it was he was happy to go with the flow—not forgetting that she could also be a useful conduit to the information he wanted.

'Don't you have the rest of your travel plans already sorted out?' Delilah was irritated to find herself lingering on the possibility that this man she had spent about fifteen seconds with might stay on for longer than he had originally suggested.

'I try not to live my life according to too many prearranged plans,' Daniel murmured, appreciating the delicate bloom of pink in her cheeks. 'I guess we probably have that in common...'

Delilah grimaced. 'I wish that *was* like me,' she said without thinking. 'But unfortunately you couldn't be further from the truth.' She reddened and spun round, away from those piercing unusual eyes. 'Of course,' she said, 'it would be lovely if you stayed on a bit longer. I'm sure you could become an able artist if you put all your efforts into it.'

She knew that the cruise ship was running at a loss. All the crew knew that. Gerry and Christine had not kept it a secret from them at all. In fact on day one they had called a meeting and apologised straight away for the fact that they couldn't be paid more. None of the teachers on board had protested. They were there because they loved what they did, and the fact that there was sun and sea in the mix was enough for all of them.

But the Ockleys had suggested that if they could try and persuade some of the passengers to prolong their stay, or even tempt interested holidaymakers into hopping on board for a couple of days to try their hand at one of the many courses… Well, every little would help.

'Persuade me over lunch,' Daniel suggested. It felt like a challenge to get her to comply—and since when had he ever backed down in the face of a challenge? 'Unless, of course, you find my company objectionable…?'

Realistically, he didn't even countenance that.

'I had lunch with you yesterday because you wanted to find out about the course.'

Delilah did her best to dredge up the memory of her disaster of a relationship with Michael and to listen to the warning voice in her head reminding her that she was still recovering from a broken heart—which, by defini-tion, meant retreating from men, taking time out, paying attention to the value of common sense.

'So? What does that have to do with anything? We've talked about the course and now I'd like to find out whether you think I'm a suitable candidate to be on it. I wouldn't want to be accused of wasting your time…so why the hesitation?'

'Perhaps a quick lunch,' she agreed—for Gerry and Christine's sake.

Daniel smiled slowly. 'Shame the choice of food is so limited,' he said, rising to his feet and giving his effort at drawing the jug a cursory glance.

If he had really been interested in learning how to draw then she would have had to commit to an indefi-nite period of time explaining to him how he might set about improving his skills, because he clearly had none.

Fortunately he had no intention of spending too long on that particular subject.

'And it's below average…'

'Sorry?' Delilah, in the act of washing her hands, turned round and frowned. 'What do you mean?'

'From what I've sampled, the food onboard doesn't exactly set the culinary world alight, does it?'

He moved to stand by the door and watched as she gathered her bag—some sort of tapestry affair that could have held the kitchen table and sink. Again, her hair was pulled back, with strands escaping round her face, and she absently shoved the stray strands behind her ear.

'It's okay…' she said cautiously.

'You don't want to rat on your fellow crew members,' Daniel murmured, with a hint of amusement in his voice. 'I understand that. But just between the two of us, I've been disappointed with what I've been served so far…'

'I don't think the passengers come for the food…'

'It's all part and parcel of the package,' Daniel said expansively. 'You said that the chef is allowed free rein…?'

'But he has to stick to a budget,' Delilah qualified uncomfortably. 'Anyway, it doesn't really matter, does it? I mean, if you're *really* unhappy, then perhaps you should mention something to Christine…'

'Who is the head chef?'

'Stan…and he works really hard to do the best he can with the money he's allotted…' She tripped along behind him, riveted by the long, lean lines of his muscular body.

'Don't worry,' Daniel said in a placating voice.

They had reached the bar and, as usual, people were tucking in to the offerings in a desultory fashion. Salads… baguettes with a variety of fillings…jacket potatoes…

It beggared belief that the owners of the liner had got their mismanagement down to such a fine art. Had they *no* concept of the importance of good food onboard a cruise liner, where the passengers did not have the option of scouting around for alternative restaurants?

'I'm not going to accost your pal in front of the chip-fryer…'

'Can I tell you something?' She reached into her bag for her wallet and insisted that she paid for his drink, as he had paid for hers the day before. This wasn't a date.

Daniel was chuffed. He couldn't remember the last time any woman had offered to pay for anything for him—not that he would have allowed it. But, no…the offer had never been made anyway. And yet this girl, who clearly bought her clothes from charity shops, was offering to buy him a drink. He was oddly touched by that. If only she knew!

His inherent cynicism quickly rose to the surface. If only she knew how much he was worth, then there was no chance in hell that she would be dipping into her wallet to buy him anything.

Once upon a time, in the tragic wake of his mother's death, he had foolishly allowed his emotions their freedom. He had fallen for Kelly Close's sympathetic ear. He had harboured no suspicions about the sweet-natured primary school teacher who had been into doing good and giving back to the community. He'd enjoyed lavishing gifts on her, enjoyed basking in her shyly endearing acceptance of whatever he bought for her.

Until he'd glimpsed the band of pure steel underneath the shyness when she had ditched her job and suggested that they make their arrangement permanent. It had occurred to him then, belatedly, that when you got past all the coy dipping of the eyes and trembling, grateful smiles, she had managed to acquire quite a substantial nest egg of priceless jewellery—not to mention the studio apartment he had bought her because the lease on her own flat had supposedly expired, and the countless weekends away.

At that point he had tried to pull back and bring some common sense to bear on the proceedings. He had discovered then that gold-diggers came in all different shapes and sizes and, his guard temporarily down, had realised that Kelly Close had found her way through the cracks in his armour and staged a clever assault, with her eventual aim being a wedding ring on her finger and a claim to his vast inheritance should they ever divorce. Which, he had seen very quickly, would have happened sooner rather than later.

A clean severing of the ways, however, had turned into a cat fight. Threats of a kiss-and-tell exposé to the tabloids had resulted in money changing hands—a vast sum of money, which had hit him at the worst possible time. In return he had managed to secure a contract with a privacy clause, prohibiting her from ever mentioning his name in public, but the emotional cost to him had also been steep.

With his brother and his father in another country, he had at least been spared the horror of either of *them* knowing about the unholy mess and the financial cost to him because he had taken his eye off the ball. But he had learnt a valuable lesson, and now, whilst it cost him nothing to be generous with his money, he made damn sure not to be generous with his emotions. Those he kept firmly under wraps. Considering his women exited their relationships with him better off by furs and diamonds and cars, he didn't think it was an unfair trade-off.

'What?' he asked.

Their eyes tangled and he didn't look away. But she was desperate to. He could see it in those sherry-coloured eyes and in her sudden flush. She wanted to look away but she was drawn to look at him.

What would she be like under those clothes? What noises did she make when she made love? What would it feel like to touch her between her legs...to hold her small breasts in his big hands...to lick her nipples...?

He cleared his throat, got a grip. He liked the fact that he never lost control when he was with a woman. *Never.* He had no idea why he kept veering off in that direction now. Was it the salty tang of the sea air? He was here on a fact-finding mission and yet he felt as though he was playing truant from real life. Was that it?

'I've known lots of art students...' She tiptoed around her words, not wanting them to sound offensive. Artists could sometimes be very sensitive souls. 'And you're nothing like any of them...'

'I'm very glad to hear it,' Daniel drawled. He immediately sideswiped a sudden twinge of guilt at his masquerade. 'I pride myself on being one of a kind.'

'That's what I mean,' Delilah blurted out. 'You'd never hear an artist come out with something as arrogant as that.' She pressed the palms of her hands against her cheeks, mortified. 'I'm so—so sorry...' she stammered.

When Gerry and Catherine had made noises about the crew trying to persuade their guests into prolonging their stay, she didn't think that one of the methods they would have advised using would have been insults. Delilah was horrified at what she had said. She was not the sort who ever did anything but encourage.

Having grown up with her wildly unorthodox background, she knew only too well the frailty of human beings—the way they could be lovable and exasperating at the same time. She had seen the way her sister had made allowances for their mum and dad, and she, too, had fallen into line, doing the same. She also knew how hurtful unintentionally blunt statements could be. Her mum had once told Sarah, without meaning to offend at all, that too much maths was turning her into a very boring person. Delilah didn't think that her sister had ever forgotten that stray remark, which had been accompanied by a merry laugh and a fond ruffling of her hair.

She impulsively rested her hand on his and Daniel looked at her earnestly.

'I think I'll survive,' he said, making no move to remove his hand.

She had beautiful fingers. Long and slim and soft—the fingers of an artist or a musician. He was tempted to ask if she played any instruments...

'In fact, you aren't the first person to have told me that I can sometimes be a little arrogant,' he confessed, with such a rueful, charming, self-deprecating smile that Delilah could feel all her bones begin to melt.

Which made her yank her hand away at the speed of light. Her heart was beating so fast that she would have bet that if everyone in the bar fell silent they would all hear it.

'But I prefer to think of it as being self-confident...' he expanded softly. 'Now, if you insist on buying a drink for me, then I will graciously accept—but on one condition...'

'What's that?' She barely recognised her voice, which sounded high-pitched, girlish and breathless. She cleared her throat. She was a teacher, being paid to do a job. He was her *pupil*. She was also sworn off men.

Her ego had been battered and bruised by her experience with Michael. She wondered whether, instead of toughening her up the way it should have, it had somehow made her more vulnerable to someone like this guy, with his smooth charm and his insanely sexy good looks... Or was he the equivalent of a strong dose of pick-me-up tonic? Was that light, musing, flirtatious banter just a soothing balm, restoring her fragile self-confidence, making her feel good about herself?

And if it was then why should she be nervous around

him? It wasn't as though she was going to actually let him get under her skin, was she? He was nothing more than a passing stranger whose innate charm made her feel better about herself.

She relaxed when she looked at it in that light. It made sense.

'I buy you dinner.'

'What for?'

'Why not?' Daniel frowned.

'You've already bought me lunch. Twice. So that we could talk about the course I offer and your contribution.' She was doggedly determined not to let a couple of non-dates and a dinner invitation—extended because he was obviously a very sociable animal, probably accustomed to an abundance of female company—go to her head. 'I don't see the point of dinner. What do you want to talk about now?'

'Good God…what sort of an answer is *that*?'

Delilah thought it was a very good answer to give a guy who was probably bored by the lack of female eye candy on the ship. A bit of mild flirting might do her the power of good, but it was important for him to realise that she wasn't easy. She was probably over-thinking the whole thing, because she knew that she was no supermodel—and he was good-looking enough to have supermodels banging on his door even if he wasn't made of money. But still…

'How old are you?' Daniel asked, while she was still in the middle of getting her thoughts together.

'Twenty-one, but…'

'We're not at *school*, Delilah… Do you mind if I call you by your first name? We're two adults on a cruise ship. I think it's fair to say that accepting a dinner invitation from me doesn't actually require hours of mental debate and indecision. It's a simple yes or no scenario…'

'Of course, but...' But why did it feel so *dangerous*? Like he said, they were both adults—and why not?

'Besides...' He leaned forward, drawing her into an intimate circle where only the two of them existed. 'I was given a little money before I...er...embarked on this adventure, and I promised myself that I would spend it buying dinner for a beautiful woman...'

Delilah felt a thrill of forbidden pleasure race through her at his blatant flattery. He was so utterly serious that she could feel herself going hot and cold. Gripped with sudden panic and confusion, she tried to remember if she had ever felt like this when she had been with Michael— or had that been more of a slow-burning attraction? The meeting of two minds, connected, she had thought at the time, at the same level? Of course he had been a very attractive man, too, but certainly not in this full-on, sledge-hammer-to-the-ribs kind of way.

Two different situations, she told herself, frowning. This was pure lust—her body reminding her that whilst her emotions had been knocked for six, she could still respond to other men. Reminding her that she would recover from the blow she had taken and that being physically attracted to another man was the first step. This was a healthy and positive reaction to someone with drop-dead good looks.

'Surely you wouldn't insult me by throwing my invitation back in my face? And I thought we could make it something a bit more special than the buffet in the restaurant...'

Daniel hadn't actually tried the buffet, but judging from what he had sampled of the other meals, he didn't think it would be too hard to top it.

'What would that be?' Delilah asked, curiosity getting the better of her.

'I'd like to see you with your hair loose,' he heard

himself say—which surprised him as much as it surprised her.

Delilah's hand flew to her hair and her eyes widened. 'I beg your pardon?'

'Tonight. Have dinner with me. Dress up...wear your hair loose... I have money to blow and I've never been one to hang on to money if I can spend it. I'm going to ask your head chef to prepare a meal especially for us, and I intend to pay him way over the odds for it. Of course I'll make sure I clear it with the captain and his...er... wife first...'

He had no doubt at all that they would accept his offer with alacrity, and it would afford him the opportunity to see exactly what standard the head chef was capable of cooking to. As with all the other members of the crew, he would be more than happy to keep the chef in gainful employment if he was up to scratch. He might be on the verge of staging a hostile takeover, but that didn't mean he couldn't be fair in certain areas.

To his complete mystification she continued to look dubious, even though he could sense that she wanted to take him up on his offer. Even though he could sense that there was a part of her that was drawn to him...

'I'd bet that Stan...that is his name, isn't it?...would love nothing more than to practise the skills he's learnt without having to consider a budget...'

'Isn't it a bit extravagant to blow a lot of money on a meal when you've still got travelling to do...? I mean, I'm assuming this is just a single leg of your journey...'

'I'm very touched by your concern,' Daniel said gently, 'but I'm more than capable of looking after my finances... So what time will you be ready to join me? It's going to be a stunning night. The water is as calm as a sheet of glass. I think I'll get a table laid out for us in a secluded corner of the deck outside... Dining under the stars has always been something of a dream for me, and when else would I be likely to get the chance?'

Delilah wondered how much money he had to spend. She couldn't fight the fact that it was incredibly flattering, and a bit of flattery was just so seductive to her at this point in time. What was the harm in responding to it? As long as she remained in control everything would be fine—and she knew that she was more than capable of remaining in control. She might not be very experienced, but she was experienced enough to know that she would never risk making an idiot of herself again.

'Just dinner,' she said quickly.

'As opposed to dinner and...what?'

Unaccustomed to this sort of sexual banter, Delilah flushed and cleared her throat. 'I don't feel comfortable accepting an invitation from you when I know that it's going to cost the earth,' she offered lamely, only just rescuing herself from launching into a ridiculous speech about sex not being on the agenda because she wasn't looking for any kind of relationship and she wasn't the sort of girl who went in for meaningless flings.

'Hardly *the earth*,' Daniel pointed out drily. 'I'll pay the going rate for a good meal in Sydney. Or London. Or New York. Plus a little extra for the setting, of course...'

He named a figure that made her eyes water.

She had no idea what it felt like to spend that much money on a single meal in one reckless go. Her parents had seldom eaten out. In fact her mother had been a terrible cook and Sarah had usually done the cooking duties in the house. Delilah could remember meals, but they had all been basic, with food bought on a budget, because her parents had never had more than a couple of dimes to rub together. And then later, at art college, she had scraped by and so had everyone else she had known.

Even when she had been going out with Michael they had gone out on the cheap.

This seemed so generous...so impulsive...so *tempting*... Would it be so very wrong to accept? Would a couple of hours of being made to feel better about herself really hurt?

'I would offer to pay half, but there's no way I could afford it,' she said—and if that was the end of that, then so be it, she thought. Though her mind was already leaping ahead to the seductive prospect of being made to feel desirable and attractive by a man like him. 'I mean, I earn... Well, not much, in actual fact...because...'

'Because they're not making much money on this liner...?'

'Times are tough,' she said vaguely. 'The economy isn't booming and cruises aren't the sort of things that people race to throw money at...'

Too true, Daniel thought wryly. Especially ill-conceived cruises with sub-standard food that only seemed to attract ageing hippies with limited disposable incomes...

He was mentally making a note of everything she said and everything he saw, because when it came to putting in an offer there was no way he would allow the Ockley couple to try and pull a fast one by pretending their cruises were anything but loss-making ventures.

'Besides...' Delilah thought of the money she was currently sending to her sister, trying to pull her weight in paying off the interest on the loan they had secured from the bank for their building work.

Daniel tilted his head to one side and looked at her narrowly. 'Besides what...?'

'Nothing. Okay. Well, why not? Dinner might be nice... And maybe,' she tacked on dutifully, 'I could persuade you to extend your stay on the ship...?'

'Maybe,' Daniel said, non-committal.

He thought that *that* kind of conversation would hit a roadblock in under thirty seconds. No, this evening would be about finding out about the cruise and her fellow crew members.

And finding out about *her*. She'd been on the verge of saying something about where her limited income went and he had to admit that he was curious. Unlike the women he had dated in the past, she was reluctant to try and engage his attention by bombarding him with every single detail about herself. That in itself fired up his curiosity.

'And you can tell me about your travels,' she said wistfully. 'Where you're planning on heading to next...'

'That's easy. London.'

'Really?'

'I have some...some business to attend to over there...'

'What do you do?' Delilah asked with interest. 'I mean, what's your profession?'

'I work in the leisure industry.'

Which was absolutely true. Although in fairness she probably wouldn't get close to suspecting the role he actually played. Not so much *working* in the industry as running and dominating it...

'That probably explains how you managed to get the time off to do a little drifting,' she said with a smile. 'I guess if you worked in an office your manager mightn't be too thrilled if you told him that you wanted time off to explore the artist in you...'

Daniel laughed. He was rarely bothered by a guilty conscience, but he couldn't help feeling another twinge of guilt at his deliberate manipulation of the truth.

'I don't have a manager,' he murmured. 'Funny, but I've always found it galling to obey someone else's orders.'

Delilah laughed, her eyes tangling with his. He was *so sexy.* He had that indefinable sexiness that came with not caring what other people thought about you. He didn't give a damn if she or anyone else thought that some of the things he said were arrogant. She got the feeling that he wouldn't care what *anyone* thought about him.

Her heart picked up speed. The way he was looking at her, his eyes narrowed and brooding, sent little thrills of pleasure racing up and down her spine.

Why shouldn't she allow herself to feel like a woman again? Surely if she didn't then Michael would end up having the last word?

Yes, Sarah had told her that she had to learn from her experience and *make sensible choices* when it came to men, and Delilah knew that her sister was right. But the sensible choice held as much attraction as a bout of flu, and wicked rebellion flared inside her.

She licked her lips in a gesture that Daniel thought was unconsciously erotic.

'No one likes taking orders from other people,' she said breathlessly. 'I guess we'd all like to be able to do our own thing, but unfortunately that's not how life is.'

Daniel looked around him before settling his gaze back on her flushed face. 'This strikes me as a pretty loose situation for you,' he pointed out. 'Didn't you tell me that you're all allowed to do your own thing on the liner, without constraints?'

'Yes, but I'm only here for a few weeks,' she reminded him.

'And then what? Going to hitch a ride on another cruise ship?'

'If only…'

Daniel leaned forward, intrigued. 'So tell me…?'

'There's nothing to tell.'

From a young age she had learnt that there were just

too many kids who were happy to snigger behind her back. She and Sarah had been the sisters with the weird parents. They'd learned that the less they'd said about their home life, the better, so they had kept themselves to themselves. The habit was so deeply engrained that even now, as a young adult, Delilah automatically shied away from confiding.

So what was it about *this* guy that made her want to open up?

And why did the thought of acting against her better judgement in accepting his invitation feel so appealing?

'I should be heading back to my cabin…' She barely recognised her voice and took a few steadying breaths. 'I… I'm going to do some preparation for my class tomorrow and…and…grab a bit of this beautiful weather… We should be at another port the day after tomorrow… It will be nice to just sit and soak up the sun with my book… You know… It's all go, go, go when we dock…and my students expect me to have clever things to say about all the places of culture that we visit…so…'

Daniel smiled slowly. 'So…' He sat back and thought that he needed to use the afternoon productively himself. Various deals going on required his attention. Time, as they said, was money. 'Seven sharp,' he murmured. 'Out on the deck. Far from the crowds…'

'You haven't got permission yet…' Delilah pointed out.

'Oh, I'll get permission,' he drawled.

'Because everyone listens and obeys when you talk?'

She'd said that jokingly, but there had been a thread of seriousness behind the jest and she wasn't all that surprised when he looked at her, eyebrows raised.

'Without exception…' he replied, deadly serious.

CHAPTER THREE

DELILAH HADN'T CATERED for dining under a starry sky with an Adonis. When she thought of guys at all now she vaguely assumed that the one meant for her would be a little dull, a little staid and a *lot* reliable. She'd had her brush with adventure and had pronounced herself jaded with love, only interested in a guy who would never use her, let her down or make inflated pie-in-the-sky promises he had no intention of keeping because he had girl-friends in every other port.

She hadn't been looking for racing pulses and sweaty excitement, and she couldn't quite believe that racing pulses and sweaty excitement had found *her*.

Consequently she possessed nothing in her wardrobe that was remotely suitable for dining with a man like Daniel. He hadn't talked about his love life, but she imagined him with lots and lots of beautiful women—the female equivalent of him. Head-turning model-types who wouldn't wear long skirts and baggy tops.

Somehow, despite his artistic inclinations, she couldn't picture him actually *going out* with an artist. At least, none of the artists *she* knew.

In the end at precisely six-thirty, after a quick shower in her cramped en-suite bathroom, she extracted the dressiest of her outfits from the single unit wardrobe.

Another long skirt, but black, and a fitted tee shirt with sleeves to the elbows—also black.

At five foot ten, she owned no high shoes at all, so she slipped on a pair of ballet pumps, giving a welcome rest to her flip-flops.

She left her hair loose.

Even in the brief length of time it had been exposed to the blistering sun it had lightened in colour. She was accustomed to tying it back. It was just more practical. Now, staring at her reflection in the mirror, she realised that the long, unruly hair she had always wished she could tame didn't look half bad.

Heart beating madly, she made her way to the outer deck to find him—she had had no idea where exactly he might be.

The sky was velvety black and pricked with tiny glittering stars. As he had said the ocean, dark and fathomless, was as still as a sheet of glass. The air was balmy, salty, indescribably fresh.

The sound of the passengers inside was barely discernible out here. There were a few couples strolling around, but most had confined themselves to the upper deck, which was more brightly lit and allowed easier access to the entertainment taking place inside.

Tonight, someone was doing a cabaret, and Delilah guiltily thought that it was a true indication of the finances of the liner that the person singing was really not terribly good—but then, as with Stan, Alfie, who was in charge of entertainment, was working on a tight budget.

Having managed to secure a charming and very secluded spot on the liner, Daniel was waiting for Delilah to track him down.

As predicted, it had been no bother getting the whole set-up arranged, and it had given him an excellent opportunity to acquaint himself with Gerry Ockley—a genial, bearded guy who clearly lacked any business acumen.

Perhaps his wife was a top-notch accountant, but Daniel doubted it.

The man had been only too happy to accept his very generous offer, and in fact had been more than willing to open up about the general finances of the liner.

Daniel brushed aside a few momentary misgivings about his planned takeover, about the fact that his aim was to get the liner at a knock-down price. When it came to business he had never felt sorry for any of the companies he had taken over. The bottom line was that a company could only be taken over if it was doing badly, and if it was doing badly then it was usually the result of bad management from the top down.

What was there to feel sorry about?

It was a dog-eat-dog world when it came to business. People got their chances, and if they screwed it up then who was to blame the predators for moving in?

But even so... On this particular occasion...

'You've found me...' He stood up, banishing unwelcome thoughts.

Delilah was staring open-mouthed at the table, the chairs, the linen cloth, the wine chilling next to him in an ice-cold bucket.

'Wow...'

'It was the best they could offer,' Daniel murmured as he pulled a chair out for her, 'given the circumstances...'

'It must have cost the earth...' She sat down and thought that it couldn't possibly get more romantic than this.

He was in a pair of dark trousers and a black polo shirt, and in the shadowy darkness he was just impossibly good-looking. When he rested those amazing eyes on her she could feel her skin tingle and her thought processes shut down. She felt like a different person...a person who was

still wonderfully alive and not nursing disillusionment…
She felt young again…

It was heady stuff, and when he poured her a glass of chilled wine she drank it far too quickly.

'Like I said… I enjoy spending money…' Which was the absolute truth—and he was generous to a fault when it came to women.

His eyes roved over her face—the full mouth, the look of fresh-faced innocence—and all of a sudden he felt impossibly jaded.

'I hope it's not money from…er…ill-gotten gains…' She could already feel that single glass of wine shoot to her head.

Daniel pretended to be outraged. 'You're not implying that I'm a *criminal*, are you?'

'No. I was just…just teasing you. It seems so wildly extravagant.'

Daniel thought that she had no idea what *wildly extravagant* entailed, and he really liked that.

'Hasn't any man ever been "wildly extravagant" with you?' he mused, and Delilah laughed.

'No!'

'Why not?'

He'd joined this cruise on a fact-finding mission, but he decided that he'd found out sufficient facts to be going on with and that it was much too tempting to find out more about the woman opposite him, blushingly sipping her wine, which he had topped up.

'Because…' She lowered her eyes and then laughed softly. 'Don't tell me you're really interested…?'

'Why wouldn't I be?'

'Because…' This flirty little game felt exotic and daring. 'Because I bet you have loads of girls scampering behind you. And men who have loads of girls scampering behind them don't really spend time listening to what they have to say.'

'I'm offended!' Daniel laughed, enjoying the conversation and the novelty of a woman who didn't care what she said to him and wasn't trying to impress.

'No, you're not.' She smiled.

'Do you have a boyfriend? And if you have why hasn't *he* done anything wildly extravagant for you?'

He fancied her. He didn't know why, because she wasn't his type, but he didn't intend to question it.

He just knew that he had spent too much of the night before thinking about her...

And she was jumpy around him—coming close and then backing away. She fancied him as much as he fancied her, and God knew she was probably wondering why—just as he was.

He thought of the sexy little number who would be waiting for him and decided on the spot that he would have to dispatch her. Right now he couldn't get his head around any other woman but the one now shyly sneaking glances at him.

'No.' She'd tensed up. 'I don't. And wildly extravagant gestures wouldn't be what I would look for in a boyfriend, anyway. I don't go for that sort of thing.'

Daniel raised his eyebrows. 'You're more into the dull-as-dishwater types? Who always make sure never to waste a single penny on something unless it has a practical purpose? You shock me, Delilah. I thought, as you're an artist, you would be wild and reckless...'

'Wild and reckless ends in tears.' She gulped down a bit more wine and realised that she was on her third glass. 'But you're teasing me, aren't you?'

'Am I?'

'My parents were wild and reckless,' she confessed.

Usually Daniel could spot the incipient beginnings

of a long-winded tale, at which point he would tactfully change the subject—because long-winded tales from women always seemed to ask for similarly long-winded tales from *him*, but this time he had no inclination to do so.

'Were they?' he encouraged.

'Sorry, I don't normally talk about myself...' She started to apologise in advance, breaking off as Stan approached, in full chef garb, to regale them with the various dishes on offer.

Daniel had been right in thinking that the chef would be thrilled to bits to cook something that wasn't dictated by a strict budget. Delilah hadn't seen him this enthusiastic since she had boarded the liner.

Choices made, Daniel sat back and looked at her expectantly.

'You were going to tell me about your wild and reckless parents?' he said.

'They were artists... Neptune and Moon.'

'Come again?' He felt his lips twitch.

'Neptune and Moon. They gave themselves those names before we were born, actually...'

'We...?'

'My sister, Sarah, and me.' She smiled. Sarah had been dismissive of their parents' crazy names, but she, Delilah, had secretly loved them because they'd sounded so ethereal and glamorous.

It suddenly clicked why she loved this cruise so much—loved working aboard the ship. It was full of people just like her parents. The formerly wild and reckless, who had been tamed only by advancing years.

Sarah, five years older, had always preached caution. She had been the mother figure, taking over where Moon had so gaily left off. She had advocated the sensible path, had kept a cautionary eye on the boys who had occasionally come to the house. And Delilah had fallen into line, turning to her sister for practical advice and to her parents for fun.

It should have been the other way around, but it hadn't been. Neither she nor her sister would have changed it for the world, but an unconventional upbringing carried its disadvantages. Maybe a yearning for fun guys was ingrained in her—like those women who just kept falling for bad boys who broke their hearts. Maybe that was why she was here, sitting in this impossibly romantic setting with this impossibly sexy guy.

It was a disturbing thought but she pushed it aside—because she wasn't going out with him. She might be having fun with someone inappropriate but she was tougher now, and not about to make the same mistake twice.

Besides, Michael had never shown any real interest in *her*—had never asked any questions about her childhood or her past. He had been a 'live for the moment' type of guy, which she could now see was part and parcel of his egocentric personality. Their conversations had all revolved around *him*—*his* exploits, *his* big plans.

'Are you going to tell me that they're on this cruise with you?' he asked drily, and she shook her head.

'My mother died five years ago,' she said quietly, 'and my father within six months afterwards. Sarah and I think it was from a broken heart. They were so attached to one another it was just inconceivable that one could exist without the other.'

'A lonely life for you kids—having parents who were so wrapped up in one another…'

She looked at him, startled. 'That's what my sister thinks, but I've never looked at it that way.'

She told him about some of the ventures her parents had been involved in, about the friends who had dropped by and remained in the cottage for weeks on end. Summer evenings when a party of three had turned into a party of ten, with someone fetching a guitar. She missed all that, even though at the time she had found it a little embarrassing—at least when compared to the very staid behaviour of her friends' parents.

She barely noticed their starters being brought for them, although she *was* aware of really enjoying what she ate.

'It's nothing *like* the stuff he cooks for the masses!'

She was relieved to get on to a less personal topic, because she found that she could have carried on blathering about herself till the cows came home. He made a good listener. *Too* good.

Too good a listener. Too good-looking a specimen. And he seemed to reach parts of her that she'd never even known existed. Sitting here, close to him, it felt as if every inch of her body was tuned in to him—as if she'd been plugged into a socket and been wired. Everything was amplified. Her breathing…the staccato beats of her heart…the little pulse in her neck… And between her legs there was a place that tingled and throbbed… It was crazy.

Daniel's keen eyes noted every minuscule reaction. She had a face that was as transparent as glass, and she was too inexperienced to have absorbed the ability to hide her emotions.

Her pupils were dilated, her full lips half parted.

Did he want to get tangled up with someone who was inexperienced? It made no sense. In fact, it defied all common sense.

But they were adults. *She* was an adult. And the way she had been looking at him for the past hour…

'What did you think of the starter?' she asked quickly, because her whole body was in danger of going up in flames.

She wondered whether it hadn't been a gigantic error

of judgement to accept this date with him. It was one thing to opt for daring and reckless and to tell herself that it was okay—because why should she continue in a deep freeze just because she had been hurt once?—but it was quite another when she had no idea what the repercussions might be.

She was vulnerable and he was dangerous.

Did that make him more exciting or less so?

Daniel sat forward, temporarily breaking the spell.

'Excellent,' he said truthfully. 'And I'm expecting the main course to be just as good. The guy obviously has a great deal of skill, even if he can't display any of it because he can't afford good ingredients…'

'It's the same with Alfie, the head of entertainment,' Delilah confided, leaning forward with a soft smile. 'He's hired a young girl to sing. Maria. But she's actually only here so that she can get in a bit of travelling before she goes to university. He plucked her when we docked in the port before Santorini. I don't think he auditioned anyone else. He doesn't have much money to play with, and I think he felt that people wanted more than just to listen to him every night on the piano… She's decorative, but way out of her depth when it comes to doing cabaret…'

'And the other teachers on the cruise? Are they as inspired as you?'

'That compliment sounds a little overblown,' she said drily, and Daniel laughed.

'You're a brilliant artist.'

'Thank you very much. I'm also very cheap, because I've only just graduated. As have a couple of the others. The rest are doing it because they love what they're teaching and don't really need the money because they're retired.'

Their main courses were brought and, as he had predicted, they were as delicious as his starter had been.

Stan, he thought, was *not* going to hit the dole queue. Little did he know it, but Stan—the chef on a budget—was about to hit the jackpot instead. Fat pay cheque and guaranteed work on the liner once it had been updated, modernised and restored to fully operational opulence.

He would find out about the remainder of the crew in his own good time. Right now he was far too absorbed in present company.

'And what are you going to do once you're through with your stint here?' he asked.

Delilah shrugged, suddenly shy of continuing the conversation, suddenly wanting him to stop right there. She was a talented artist who should be finding that the world was her oyster. Not a talented artist who would be returning to the middle of nowhere to bury herself in country life, trying to make ends meet so that the she and her sister could keep the cottage on, walking the sensible path because she had been burnt once.

'Who knows?' she said gaily. 'What about you?'

'I told you… London for me. At least for a month or so. I have a family visit to make…and work to be done… and then Australia…'

'What family visit?' she asked with interest.

London… He would bum around and make some money there, she reckoned, before taking an adventurous path to the other side of the world, seeing lots of exotic and interesting places in between.

'My brother has just found true love and become engaged…'

For a second she frowned at the tone of his voice. 'Why do you sound so cynical?'

'Learning curve…' he said neutrally. 'It's a beautiful thing.'

Theo was about to marry a girl from a similar background and so, Daniel knew, would he. Not because he was in any danger of having his relationship arranged for him, as his brother's had been—against his will—but because he knew what it felt like to get involved with someone who only had your bank balance in mind. A wealthy woman was an independent woman. There would be no danger of opportunism. Which was why it was fine for him to fool around with sexy little starlets and aspiring glamour models—there was no way any of them would make it past the starting post.

He'd loved and been hurt, Delilah thought with a little stab. And he wasn't about to launch into an emotional explanation. The shutters had dropped and for a second she'd been locked out. She'd just finished telling him all about herself and now she realised that she barely knew a thing about *him*.

'Are you close to your brother?' she asked, reluctantly eating the last tasty morsel of steak on her plate. 'What about your parents? Do they worry about you having such a nomadic lifestyle?'

Daniel had the grace to flush. 'Close to my brother? Yes. Always have been. Parents? Just my father. My mother died several years ago.'

He didn't bother with the *nomadic lifestyle* assumption because he had to have the least nomadic lifestyle on the planet. Yes, he travelled—but rarely simply for pleasure. And when he did travel for pleasure it was for very brief windows of time during which he didn't laze around and relax. He stretched himself and his body to the max.

'And what does your brother do?' She tried and failed to imagine what his brother looked like. Surely not nearly as drop-dead gorgeous?

'He's…er…in business…'

Delilah laughed that melodic laugh that made him want to smile.

'Sounds like your family is the exact opposite of my

own,' she said, waving aside the coffee that had been brought to them but tucking in to some of the chocolates. 'Although Sarah's very traditional.'

She leant in to confide in him.

'Right now she's supervising some work that's due to begin on the cottage where we live. Where we've always lived, actually. Our parents were hopeless with all things financial, and since they died we've been struggling just to make ends meet. Thank goodness Sarah is practical. She studied business at college, and if it weren't for the money she makes doing the books for some of the local businesses, well... Of course I send as much money back to her as I can, and it's been brilliant that I've managed to get hold of some work so soon after leaving art college...'

Daniel said nothing. What was there to say? He was here to buy the liner on which she worked in order to send money back to keep her home fires from being snuffed out.

'I'm talking too much about myself...' Delilah reddened. How could she have let herself get so carried away? Why would this gorgeous guy, travelling the world with only his backpack for company, be interested in *her* mundane family history? 'Can I ask you something?'

Daniel fixed watchful eyes on her. She knew nothing about his background, the immense wealth that was attached to the De Angelis name, but he was always wary of the unexpected. He had a feeling that she would not conform to type. He could economise with the truth, but it would be a harder task to lie to her outright.

'You can ask whatever you like,' he drawled. 'Just so long as I reserve the right to say *no comment.*'

Her brows pleated in a frown, because that seemed a peculiar response, but she shrugged it aside and smiled. 'I know we've only just met, but...'

She hesitated on an indrawn breath and for a second Daniel felt a twinge of disappointment.

He'd liked her shyness, the way she blushed and looked away when he stared at her for too long. He'd liked the way she didn't advertise her availability. He was so accustomed to women coming on to him that it had appealed to him that she hadn't. It had nothing to do with money. She thought he was some kind of loser—a drifter bumming around from one destination to the next with no discernible income.

No, she hadn't come on to him even though he knew without a trace of vanity that he was good-looking. Now he wondered if it had all been a ploy she would use to seduce him.

'But…?' he queried, his voice a shade cooler.

'I wondered whether I could paint you.'

Surprise deprived him of an immediate answer, allowing her time to rush into hasty speech.

'I don't mean that I want you to sit for the class,' she elaborated.

Daniel immediately relaxed. 'I'm breathing a sigh of relief even as you say that.'

'And it would have to be out of my working hours, of course. It's a huge imposition, but I think you'd make an amazing…er…subject to try and capture on canvas…'

'I'm flattered,' Daniel murmured, enjoying her obvious discomfort over making the simple request.

'You have very good bone structure,' she informed him quickly.

'I don't think any woman's ever used *that* as a chat-up line with me before…'

'I wasn't chatting you up.'

Hot and flustered, Delilah dived into the remainder of her wine and wondered whether she would be able to walk in a straight line by the time they left the table.

'Please feel free to say no. It was just an idea, but it would entail you having to waste some of the gorgeous sunshine while you pose for me. I know that you only plan on being on this cruise for a few days, and you probably don't want to waste your precious time sitting still...'

'I've always found sitting still difficult,' Daniel agreed. 'But in this instance I'm willing to make an exception.'

She smiled at him with open delight.

'But of course,' he said slowly, watching her face with leisurely thoroughness, 'there is such a thing as quid pro quo. I sit for you and in return you do something for me...'

'If it's to return your dinner invitation in a similar fashion, then there's no chance of that happening.' She laughed.

'I really like the way you laugh,' Daniel said, distracted. 'Your face lights up.'

'I don't think any man has ever used *that* chat-up line with me before...' She parroted what he had said earlier, at which point she realised that she had definitely drunk too much. She *had* to have drunk too much, because this was outrageous flirting—and outrageous flirting was something she had never done...not even with Michael...and it was something she definitely shouldn't be doing now.

Daniel looked at her with lazy intensity. She was as skittish as a cat on a hot tin roof and the urge to take her, to make love to her, ripped through him with astounding force.

He was used to getting what he wanted without putting much effort in. Women went to ridiculous lengths to get his attention. They threw themselves at him with shameful abandon. He couldn't remember the last time he'd had to work at trying to get a woman into bed, but right now, even knowing from the blush on her cheeks that she fancied him, he still hesitated.

He was almost tempted to indulge in that rarely prac-

tised art form known as *courting*, but time wasn't on his
side and he wasn't even sure if he could subdue the force
of his desire in order to take things slowly, one step at
a time.

'What do you want me to do?' she pressed on.

The sultry night air… The black ocean all around
them… The stars above… She was on a high.

'I'll tell you in a little while.'

He tossed his linen napkin on to his plate and looked
around to see Stan, peering at them anxiously from behind the glass windows.

Delilah could only gape as he beckoned the chef across
with a practically invisible inclination of his head, but
she was thrilled when he proceeded to compliment him
on everything they had been served. Thrilled when he
quizzed him about his background in cooking, apparently
interested in hearing all about where Stan had trained and
what had brought him to the liner.

Dnaiel might not divulge a lot about himself, but somehow his restraint was a…

A turn-on…

Compared to him, Michael—who had always been
eager to promote himself and had never tired of talking
about the exciting life he'd lived, taking photographs in
exotic places—seemed immature and empty.

Somehow Daniel didn't glory in his exploits.

He was clearly used to dealing with different people
of different cultures and in different situations, but his
anecdotes weren't laced with self-praise. It was odd that
she was only now fully recognising that trait in Michael,
seeing him for what he really was, and it felt good—like
an achievement.

'Are you *sure* you can afford this?' she whispered,
when Stan had eventually cleared the table and left, vis-
ibly puffed up by Daniel's effusive praise.

'Have you *never* been wined and dined before?' He laughed, standing up and waiting for her to get to her feet.

'Do fast food restaurants count?'

He laughed, reached for her hand and tucked it into the crook of his elbow.

Delilah's state of heightened excitement escalated a couple of notches. She could feel the ripple of sinew and muscle in his forearm and the outside lights danced over his face, throwing it into wildly exotic angles.

They strolled towards the railings and peered down at the endless ocean.

This had been a bloody good idea, Daniel thought, with a feeling of wellbeing. *Inspired*, in fact. He hadn't banked on any sort of sexual entanglement, but now that the possibility had surfaced he certainly wasn't going to run away from it.

But first things first…

He turned round so that he was leaning against the railing, with his back to the ocean, and pulled her gently towards him. He registered an initial resistance before she yielded, although her body remained stiff.

'Relax,' he urged, with a smile in his voice.

'You should know something,' Delilah said in a rush. 'I've just come out of a relationship and it didn't end very well. So I'm not… I'm not looking for anything… I shouldn't be doing this at all…'

'You're not doing anything.'

'I'm here…on a date…with *you*…'

'What did he do?'

'He strung me along,' she said painfully.

'That,' said Daniel, 'is something I would never do. I've always made it a policy to lay my cards on the table, and when it comes to women I don't string them along. If you're not looking for a relationship, trust me—neither am I. This is a harmless attraction.'

He was right—*so why didn't it feel that way?* she wondered.

'Harmless?'

'No strings attached,' he soothed. 'And without strings attached there's no emotional involvement. It's only when emotions are in the mix that complications begin. I've been there, done that, and I'm a convert to the uncomplicated arrangement...'

He made it sound so easy, and his conviction liberated her from her misgivings. Who cared whether it was a good idea or a bad idea? She could spend all night analysing the rights and wrongs and then he'd be gone, and she knew that she would regret not having had the courage to take what he was offering.

And wasn't he just echoing what she had been thinking anyway? He'd been upfront and honest with her. He was passing through and she was here, in a bubble, with no one looking over her shoulder.

She tentatively wrapped her arms around him, glad that it was deserted on this section of the deck.

'I'm only here for a few days, Delilah...'

'I know that.'

'You'll only be able to paint me for those few days.'

'I know that, too.'

'And here's where I get to the thing I want from you in return for sitting for you...'

'Yes?' Her voice was a breathy whisper.

'You. I want *you*, Delilah...'

There was just no way that bluntly spoken statement could be invested with anything romantic at all, and yet...

It went to her head with like an injection of adrenaline directly into her bloodstream.

'That's the trade?' she framed in a shaky voice.

'Never let it be said that I don't know how to strike a deal while the iron's hot...'

He dipped his head and his lips met hers in an unhurried, all-consuming kiss. His tongue meshed with hers and it was the most erotic experience she had ever had. Even though his hands remained clasping the rail on either side of him…even though it was only that long, lazy kiss that was doing the damage.

Delilah stroked the side of his lean, beautiful face and heard herself say, *'Okay…'*

CHAPTER FOUR

DELILAH HAD NO idea how she managed to focus at all the following day. Her routine had been disrupted by the liner putting in to dock at Olympia.

Before Daniel had boarded the cruise ship she had diligently looked at the itinerary and made copious notes about all the exciting places of cultural interest they would be visiting. Part of her responsibilities covered introducing interested passengers to new experiences. Bearing in mind she had not travelled at all, and that every single sight would be as fresh to her as to them, she had worked doubly hard to make sure that she had all the relevant facts and figures at her disposal.

Olympia...site of the Olympic Games in classical times...held every four years from the eighth century BC to the fourth century AD...all in honour of the great god Zeus...

She had done all her homework on the Greek gods and Greek mythology. She could have passed an exam.

But as it was, the only thing filling her head as they disembarked was the guy who had allowed her to scuttle back to her cabin the evening before alone, with just a chaste kiss on her cheek as a reminder of his lips.

'You need to think about my proposal...' he had

drawled in his dark, sexy voice, while his eyes had remained fastened to her face, draining her of all her willpower. 'I need to know that we're going to be on the same page…'

He didn't do long-term. He didn't do commitment. He wasn't looking for a relationship. He was looking for a bit of fun and he wanted his fun to be with *her*…

The thought of the *having fun and clearing off* situation he was proposing should have left her stricken with terror after Michael, but she had squared away her misgivings. Daniel had been right when he'd said that no one could get hurt when emotions weren't involved—that was true.

Desire, as she was finding out fast, was a stand-alone emotion. That had come as a revelation to someone who had always thought of love and desire in the same breath. She wanted him, he wanted her, and there was something so wonderfully clean and clear-cut about that. It was nothing like the muddle of hopes and dreams and forward-planning she had so foolishly felt with Michael.

Right here and right now this was liberating.

Now, in the bright, burning sun, Daniel was part of the group she had opted to show around the ancient ruins. How was she supposed to deliver her spiel when she could feel his eyes following her every move? Could see him listening to every word she said with his head tilted?

He was the very picture of keen amateur interest—even though, unlike some of the others, he had not brought his sketchpad with him. Notwithstanding that, she knew what was running through his head. She could just *tell* whenever their eyes met and his gaze lingered on her.

She and Daniel would share a cabin bed for a few days and then he would disappear for ever.

He hadn't even tried to package up the deal in attractive wrapping paper.

He had told it like it was—told her to expect nothing more.

He was a textbook example of just the sort of guy she should be avoiding. No promise of anything long-term. No mention of love.

But she had underestimated the force of her own body and the way it was capable of responding to something that made no sense.

She would return to the Cotswolds, where she could count eligible guys on the fingers of one hand, and she would settle down with someone more suitable. Of course she would. There would be all the time in the world for her to invest her love in Mr Right. But how would she feel if she did that and always thought about the Mr Wrong she had decided to avoid? The Mr Wrong who would be just the sort of replacement therapy she was in need of?

The group lunched at a charming little café close to the site they had been exploring and later, with the sun still burning down, late in the afternoon, made their way back to the liner.

'I'm disappointed you didn't take your sketchpad with you.' She turned to Daniel once they were back on the liner, joining all the others also making their way back on and then dispersing into various groups, or going to one of the bars to relax before the evening meal.

It had been a hot, tiring day, but he still managed to look amazing. In a plain white tee shirt, some khaki shorts, loafers and sunglasses, he looked like one of the Greek statues come to beautiful life.

'I thought about it, but then concluded that I would have much more fun watching you.'

He couldn't credit the level of his excitement at the prospect of sleeping with her. The detailed report he had been putting together, which would highlight all the reasons why the Ockley couple would find themselves without an option when it came to selling to him, had taken a back seat.

For the first time in living memory work wasn't uppermost in his mind.

Delilah, captivated by the slow-burning desire she could see in the depths of his green eyes, was finding it hard to tear her gaze away.

'I… I should go and change… Have a look at some of the sketches my class have done…'

'Boring.'

'I beg your pardon?'

'Give me the sketches and I'll mark them out of ten. Even without the benefit of a degree in art I could tell you that Miranda and Lee need to pay more attention in perspective class…'

Her lips twitched and she struggled not to laugh. 'Maybe I could meet you…later…?'

Daniel leant against the wall, drawing her into an intimate circle that enclosed just the two of them, and Delilah looked shiftily around her.

'We're not breaking any laws,' he said, with an edge of impatience.

'Yes, I know. But…'

'But what? So *what* if some of the people in your class think that we're having a fling? What do you think they're going to do? Report you to the principal?'

'It's not that,' she said sharply. 'The fact is that I'll be staying on after you leave this liner, and I don't want to have people whispering about me behind my back.'

Daniel raked his fingers through his hair and shook his head. 'Why do you care what people think?'

'Don't you?'

'Of course not. No, I tell a lie. I care about what my father and my brother think of me, but beyond that why should I?' Their eyes met, and when she dipped her head to look away he tilted it back so that she was looking at him, his finger gently on her chin. 'Okay,' he conceded, 'why don't you tell me where you are and I'll come to you under cover of darkness…like a thief in the night…'

'Tell you where I am…?' Her mouth went dry at the thought of that, in a mixture of excitement and nervousness.

'Your cabin?' he said drily. 'Unless you're bunking down in a sleeping bag out on the deck?'

'I…'

'Are you having second thoughts?' *Because,* he might have added, *there's a limit to the amount of chasing I intend to do.* He'd never had to chase. Frankly, an attack of nerves—the whole three steps forward, two steps back thing—was something he could do without.

But he wasn't sure whether his rampant libido was capable of walking away.

'No, I'm not having second thoughts.' Delilah had made up her mind and she wasn't going to backtrack.

He smiled and found himself relaxing, which only made him realise that he'd tensed up at the thought of her changing her mind.

'But…' She sighed.

'You're nervous?' he intuited, and she looked at him sheepishly. 'You're not the kind of girl who accepts propositions from strange men you meet on cruise liners…? And especially not when you're supposedly recovering from a broken heart…'

'I was in love with the idea of *being* in love,' she said slowly. 'I wanted excitement and adventure, and when Michael came along it felt like I'd found that…'

'Rule number one,' Daniel drawled, 'is that you don't talk about your ex when you're with me. He's history—and good riddance from the sound of it.'

'Is that the approach you took when *your* heart was broken?' she asked tentatively.

'Another rule—we don't talk about my exes either. But, just for your information, my heart wasn't broken. The bottom line is that whatever doesn't kill you makes you stronger.'

'You're so…so *confident*…' Delilah was frankly in awe of his pragmatic approach.

Daniel shrugged coolly. 'You don't get anywhere by dithering or dwelling on past errors of judgement. You learn and you move on.'

'When you say stuff like that it shows me how much I don't know about you… I mean, I don't know anything other than you're travelling and your next stop is London before you head off to the other side of the world…'

But then she'd thought she'd known Michael because he had talked a lot about himself, and she hadn't at all, had she?

'What else do you want to know? And do you want to have this long and meaningful conversation over there?' He nodded to the outer deck and to a clump of deckchairs, all of which were empty.

Did she want more facts about him? Delilah felt that she knew *the essence* of the man, and knew that she had been drawn to him not just because of the way he looked but because he was incredibly funny, incredibly intelligent and so thoughtful and considerate in the way he had listened to her without interruption. The way he was interested in everything she had to say.

'I have a very small cabin,' she said shyly. 'All of the crew do…'

'Then come to me,' Daniel murmured. 'I can't say it's a palatial suite, but there's a double bed… My feet have a tendency to hang over the edge, but they probably don't cater for men as big as me… And don't be nervous. Who says I'm accustomed to picking up strange girls I meet on cruise liners…?'

'Are you telling me that *you're* nervous?'

'I can say with my hand on my heart that I have never been nervous when it comes to sex…'

'You're so…so…'

'I know what you're going to say. You're going to tell me that I'm so *arrogant*—I prefer the *confident* description.'

Delilah laughed, and just like that he kissed her. And this time his kiss wasn't lingering and explorative. This time it was hungry and demanding.

He manoeuvred her so that they had stepped outside onto the deck and his mouth never left hers.

She'd been kissed before, but never like this, and she'd never felt like this before either. His hunger matched hers and she whimpered and coiled her fingers into his hair, pulling him into her and then arching her head back so that he could kiss her neck, the side of her face, the tender spot by her jawline.

Her whole body was on fire, and right here, right now, she couldn't have cared less who saw her.

She lost the ability to think, and along with her ability to think, she also lost her inhibitions. She'd taken her time with Michael, wanting to make sure that they had something really lasting and special before she slept with him, and it was puzzling that she just wanted to fly into bed with Daniel even though there was nothing between them but lust.

She couldn't get enough of him, of his mouth on her mouth, on her bare skin, setting her aflame. She wanted to touch. Was *desperate* to touch. Not just his beautiful face but all of him. And she was shocked by the need pouring through her in a tidal wave that eclipsed every preconceived notion she had ever had about the nature of relationships.

When he pulled away she actually moaned—a soft little broken moan—before reluctantly opening her eyes and staring right up at him.

'You're beautiful,' Daniel told her roughly, and Delilah laughed shakily.

'I bet you say that to all the women you chase...'

'I don't chase women.'

'Because they chase *you*?'

Daniel smiled slowly, his silence telling her that she had hit the nail on the head. He was a man who didn't have to run after women. He was a guy who didn't have to try.

He was a guy who probably needed someone who played hard to get—but she wasn't good at playing games, and besides this wasn't a normal relationship...was it?

This wasn't one of those relationships that was built to last from its foundations up. There wasn't going to be a slow burn, or a gradual process of discovering one another and really getting to know one another. That had been *her* learning curve, and what a fool she'd been.

This wasn't what she had spent her formative years expecting.

This was a blast of the unexpected, powering through her and obliterating all the signposts she had always taken for granted when it came to relationships.

'And you wonder why I'm nervous...' she sighed on a heartfelt whisper.

If he knew that she had never slept with a man before then he would run a mile. Men who were in danger of being knocked down by the stampede of women eager to climb into bed with him would have no concept of an inexperienced woman, and they wouldn't have any patience with one.

She didn't want him to run a mile.

Just acknowledging that shocked her, but she was honest enough not to flinch from the truth.

This was pure lust, and sleeping with him felt necessary and inevitable.

'Don't be,' he told her softly. 'Just because women chase me it doesn't mean that I make comparisons... Now, I'm going to go and have a much needed shower, and my cabin number is...'

He whispered it into her ear and she shivered.

Just the fact that they were pre-planning this sent a delicious frisson rippling through her.

She almost didn't want him to leave, but she was hot and sticky as well.

She watched him disappear back into the body of the liner and her heart was thudding so hard in her chest that she wanted to swoon like a Victorian maiden.

Delilah had no idea what a man who looked like Daniel saw in her, but she made sure to do her utmost to look her very best before she joined him in his cabin.

He liked her hair, so she left it loose and blow-dried it into glossy waves. She wore no make-up aside from some mascara and a little lip gloss, and thankfully the sun had turned her skin a pale biscuit-brown. As for clothes...

Instead of her usual long skirts she wore one of the only two pairs of trousers she had brought with her. Having anticipated a shorter stay on the liner, she'd found her scant supply of clothes had had to stretch for far longer than she'd bargained for, but these tan trousers hadn't yet seen the light of day and they looked okay, twinned with a cropped vest that showed off her slender arms and just a sliver of tanned belly.

When she stood back from the mirror she realised that

the artist had gone—at least for the night. She briefly wondered whether he might have preferred her artist image, but swatted that temporary misgiving away.

Nerves took hold of her as she made her convoluted way to his cabin. Many of the rooms were empty, waiting for the occasional new passenger who might want to hop on board—not that there had been very many of those, despite the brilliant deals advertised. And she knew, as she wound her way to his section of the ship, that he was in one of the best cabins—probably an upgrade.

Gerry and Christine were generous to a fault, and most of the passengers had been offered upgrades at very little extra cost.

She could barely breathe as she tentatively knocked on the door, pushing it open as he told her to enter.

Outside, darkness had abruptly fallen, another starry, moonlit night, and through the portholes of his cabin she could see the stars twinkling in the sky and the whisper of a crescent moon illuminating the sea with a ghostly radiance.

He'd changed into cream trousers, low slung on his lean hips, and a cream tee shirt, and he was barefoot.

Delilah discovered that she was finding it hard to catch her breath and the Victorian maiden swoony feeling was beginning to get hold of her again.

She inhaled deeply and made a conscious effort not to twist her hands together in a giveaway gesture of nervousness.

God, he was beautiful. That streaky dirty blond hair was slightly too long but somehow emphasised the sharp contours of his face, adding depth to the fabulous green eyes and accentuating the bronzed skin tone that spoke of some exotic heritage in his gene pool. No wonder he needed to carry a large stick with him at all times to fight the women off.

'Are you going to tear yourself away from the door any time soon?' Daniel strolled towards her and gently propelled her into the cabin and closed the door behind her.

He'd taken one very long, very cold shower, and even that hadn't been able to stanch the unfamiliar excitement of anticipation. Always in control, he had now surrendered to the novelty of *not* being in control. The unread email messages on his computer remained unread. His mobile phone was switched off so that he wouldn't be interrupted by someone wanting something from him. His attraction to her had happened so fast and hit him so hard that he could only blame the fact that he was far removed from his comfort zone of wealth and luxury.

'You've ordered room service?' Delilah finally managed to croak as she stared down at the table, which had been set for two.

'Stan again rose to the occasion. Of course I could have just ordered something from the room service menu. but...' He shrugged, unable to tear his eyes away from her.

She'd always hidden the glorious figure he'd glimpsed beneath her baggy clothes. Even earlier, when they had visited the site of the ruins, she had worn a long skirt and flip-flops and yet another loose, floaty top. 'It's the best thing if you want to keep cool,' she had told him when he had asked her whether she wasn't scared of tripping over her skirt and doing untold damage as they clambered around.

She wasn't wearing camouflage gear now.

Caramel skin...those strangely captivating eyes... long russet hair tamed into sexy waves...so, so...long. Way too long to be fashionable, but incredibly, *incredibly* spectacular...

And she wasn't wearing a bra. He could see the firm roundness of her small breasts pushing against the thin, tight vest. Could practically see the circular outline of her nipples...

Feeling as hot and bothered as a horny teenager on his first date, he spun away and reached for the bottle of champagne which was chilling in an ice bucket.

'And—and bubbly,' she stammered, watching him expertly open the bottle. 'You didn't have to...to go to all this trouble...' She fiddled with the thin gold chain she wore round her neck—a birthday present from her parents a million years ago.

'Allow a man to be indulgent...' He held out a champagne flute to her, but before she could drink he curved his hand over her satin-smooth cheek and watched her for a few seconds without saying anything.

'You're staring...' Delilah breathed, but the feel of his hand on her was strangely calming.

'You do that to me,' Daniel husked. 'You make me want to stare.'

He'd always gone for the obvious in women—much to his brother's perpetual amusement. Plenty of time to settle for the prissy, classy clothes of the wealthy, well-bred woman of means he would eventually marry. Prissy and classy wasn't fun, and in the meanwhile he intended to have a fun-filled diet.

This woman couldn't have been more restrained in her choice of clothing, but the effect on him was dramatic.

Delilah sipped the champagne and watched him warily over the rim of her glass. Wanting to be here didn't mean that she had the courage to match her desire.

'I thought we'd have something light to eat.' Daniel broke the bubble of heightened silence and pulled out a chair for her. 'Unless you've already grabbed something? No? Thought not...'

She was still nervous. That in itself was a bad sign, because it meant that she wasn't exactly into transitory sex—which was what he wanted—despite what she'd said. But he had given her his speech and that had been sufficient to ease his conscience.

Both adults and due warning. Job done.

Which nevertheless still left the fact that she was nervous, and he found that he was willing to go against the grain, willing to move at her pace within reason. In a peculiar way, he was willing to court her…

'Stan has prepared salad stuff…crayfish and lobster… two things that go perfectly with champagne…'

Delilah sat. Her eyes were fairly popping. What had she expected? Not this. Maybe she'd thought that he would greet her half naked at the door, Tarzan-style, before slinging her over his shoulder and heaving her off to his bed. There was, after all, something raw and elemental about him.

He might not be on the lookout for any kind of relationship, but he was putting a lot of effort in, and she knew instinctively that he was taking things slowly because he sensed that she was nervous.

And that warmed her, because it said so much about him.

'He'll miss you when you go,' she said lightly, helping herself to salad, the little pulse in her neck fluttering with awareness as he sat down opposite her.

His cabin was at least five times the size of hers. It was comfortable, but not luxurious, and even with her untrained eyes she could see the hallmarks of Gerry and Christine's straitened financial circumstances. The room needed a good overhaul.

Through the doorway she could glimpse the bed, and she quickly averted her eyes, determined not to become a victim of stage fright.

'You've spoiled him by letting him cook whatever he wants, no expense spared…'

'Are you going to deliver another sermon on my extravagance?'

Delilah blushed. 'No, I'm not. You're not careful, and that's nice. My sister and I have spent so long just trying to make ends meet that I've become accustomed to being careful all the time when it comes to money.'

'You spend a lot of time talking about your sister...'

Excellent salad, he mentally noted. Another point in Stan's favour—and his sous chef as well. Two jobs safe. And from what he'd seen some of the rest of the crew were diligent and efficient and, having spoken to them, he'd seen they knew the ropes.

'She brought me up,' Delilah said simply.

'And where were your parents when this sisterly bringing up was taking place?'

He was fascinated by the guileless transparency of her face. She smiled, dipped her eyes, blushed, fiddled with her champagne flute... Her broken heart hadn't been able to kill off her naturally warm, shy disposition.

Was it unreasonable to expect his next woman to have those appealing traits?

Then he remembered that this woman knew nothing about him. She wasn't out to impress him. He felt that had she known just how wealthy, how powerful, how influential he was, she would probably be a lot more forward in trying to grab his attention and hold it.

'Like I said, our parents were so wrapped up in one another that they didn't have a lot of time for us. I mean, they were fabulous parents, and very, very loving in their own scatty way, but they were unconventional. They really didn't see the point of school.' Delilah smiled. 'Despite the fact that they both went to art college. They had a lot of faith in the University of Life.'

'But they were fun?' Daniel guessed.

'Gosh—absolutely. On the one hand it was embarrassing when I was a kid, because of the way they dressed, but on the other hand they weren't all buttoned up like the rest of the parents…and that was kind of great…'

Daniel pushed back his chair and linked his fingers behind his head.

Every scrap of his attention was focused on her and Delilah could feel herself wanting to open up, like a bud blossoming under the warmth of sudden sunshine.

'And you're looking for the same kind of overpowering love…? You thought you'd found it, and it turned out that you hadn't, but that hasn't really put you off, has it?'

'Security, stability…those are the things that are important in a relationship…'

'Because you fell for the wrong guy? Because your sister told you so?'

'No! Maybe… Well, not in so many words…'

'But deep down you're not falling for it. That's why you're here with me. Deep down you don't see why you shouldn't have the fireworks and the explosions…which is what your parents had…'

'You don't understand. They really were *so* involved in one another. There'd be days when Mum would just forget to shop for food, and Sarah was always the one who shouldered the responsibility for bringing a bit of normality into the house… Sometimes, they would get one of their friends to babysit us for a week or so, while they went on a hunting mission for crystals or artefacts, and at least once a year they blew what little money they'd managed to make on a trip to India…you know, to bring stuff over for the shop…'

Neptune and Moon, Daniel thought wryly. The names said it all.

But the sisters had seen the situation through different eyes. It was obvious that sister number one was a practical bore, who had drilled into sister number two the importance of being earnest and then really hammered it home when Delilah had strayed off the tracks…

And then quite suddenly he thought about his own situation.

Theo, he knew, had been affected by the relationship of their parents and by their mother's death in ways that he, Daniel, perhaps hadn't. They'd both been devastated, had both witnessed their father's slow, inexorable decline— the way the energy had been sapped out of him, the way he had withdrawn from active life, unable or unwilling to cope after the rock on whom he had depended had been taken from him.

That had toughened Theo and shown him a road he would make sure to avoid—the road that led to any sort of emotional commitment.

Daniel couldn't help grinning at the way *that* particular situation had eventually played out, considering his brother was now loved up, locked down and proud of it.

He, Daniel, had found solace in the wake of their mother's death and the sudden upheaval in their household in another way. He had buried his emotions so deeply after Kelly Close that he doubted he would ever be able to find them again. That suited him.

Taken aback by that rare bout of introspection, he closed his hand over Delilah's and slanted her a devastating smile.

'Word to the wise?' he said wryly. 'Your sister's probably got the hang of it by steering you clear of all those fairytale stories of Prince Charmings sweeping lonesome Cinderellas off their feet so that they can live happily ever after in that mythical place known as cloud nine… Have fun and then marry the guy who makes sense.'

Was that his way of reiterating his warning? Of telling her that she had to look elsewhere for romance? She'd already got that message, and there was no way she would be idiotic enough to look for it with someone like *him*. Oh, no.

But, yes, she *did* believe in all that burning fireworks and explosions stuff—even if her sister didn't… It might be called lust, and not love, but she still wanted it and he was right—that was why she was here with him now.

Surprised by just how much she had confided in him, and made uneasy by her lack of restraint, she took a deep breath and caught his eyes.

'I didn't come here to talk,' she murmured huskily.

This, Daniel thought, was more like it. This was the kind of language he understood.

He stood up, pulled her to her feet and slowly drew her against him. 'I like the outfit, by the way…'

He kissed her long and slow, until her whole body was melting. His tongue, meshing lazily with hers, was doing wonderful things, making her want to press herself against him so that there wasn't an inch of space between their bodies. He curved his hand over her bottom and then loosely slipped it underneath the waistband of her trousers, just a few delicate fingers running against her skin.

'And I'm going to like it even more when you're out of it and it's lying on the ground…'

CHAPTER FIVE

SHE FALTERED AS he led her towards the bed she had glimpsed through the door that separated the small sitting area from the sleeping area.

Her mouth went dry and she hesitated—watched, fascinated by his complete lack of inhibition, as he began to undress.

He'd done this lots of times. There was certainty in the way he pulled the tee shirt over his head, exposing his hard, muscled torso, and self-confidence in the way he kept his eyes on her, a half smile playing on his mouth. He was a man who, as he had told her, had never been nervous when it came to sex.

This was his playing ground and he was the uncontested master of it.

Her eyes followed his hand as it reached for the zipper of his trousers and rested there for a few seconds.

'This,' he drawled, strolling towards her, 'is beginning to feel a little one-sided…'

Her courage disappearing faster than water draining down a plughole, Delilah gulped.

'Shall we get into bed?' she whispered, by which she meant under the covers, where she could wriggle out of her clothes in as inconspicuous a manner as possible.

Daniel raised his eyebrows and placed both hands on her shoulders.

They'd spent so much time talking—way more than

he had ever spent talking with any woman, and certainly way more than he had ever spent with any woman before sex. In fact, when he thought about it, conversation rarely served as an appetiser before the main course. Usually by the time he and whatever hot date he happened to be with hit the bedroom clothes would have been off and action would be about to happen—no exchange of words needed.

Hot, hard and urgent.

When, he wondered, were her nerves going to be banished? He'd had an erection from the second she'd walked into the cabin and he was in danger of having to have a very cold shower if he was to get into anything resembling a comfortable state.

'I like my women to be naked *before* we get into bed,' he said gently. 'Jumping into the sack with someone who's fully clothed, right down to her shoes, somehow takes the edge off the whole business… In other words it's a mood-killer…'

He slipped his hands under her tee shirt and Delilah tensed.

'I don't like games when it comes to sex,' he told her, his voice cooling by the second, because her body was as rigid as a plank of wood. 'I have no time for any woman who thinks that she can tease me and then pull away…'

'That's not what I'm doing.'

'Then would you care to explain why you've suddenly turned into a statue?'

Delilah dropped her head and was grateful for her long, loose hair, because it shielded her face from his piercing eyes.

'I've never done this before…' She reluctantly looked up at him with clear eyes and Daniel frowned.

'When you say that you've *never* done this before…'

'You're my first,' she told him bluntly, waiting for him to recoil in horror—but he didn't. Although she had no idea what he was thinking, because when their eyes tangled again she could see that the shutters had dropped.

'You're telling me that you're a virgin?'

'It's not *that* unusual,' she flared defiantly.

'But you were involved with someone...'

'I... We...we were taking it slowly. Look, I don't want to talk about this—'

'Too bad. You're a virgin, Delilah.' He raked frustrated fingers through his hair. 'I don't do virgins.'

'You don't *do* a lot of stuff, do you?' She found that she couldn't bear the thought of him walking away from her—not after she had convinced herself that this was the right thing to do, the thing she wanted and needed to do. 'Why don't you just come right out and say it? You're just not attracted to me now!'

She made to turn away but his grip was holding her in place. He was holding her very gently, applying almost no pressure, but he was strong. *Very* strong.

'Touch me and you'll see that for the nonsense it is,' he told her roughly.

She fixed her eyes on his hard chest—his small, flat brown nipples, the dark gold hair spiralling down to where he had begun unbuttoning his trousers before stopping.

Heat poured through her, settling damply between her legs.

Her eyes flared and, feeling her very slight tremble, Daniel knew that what he should do right now was gently let her go. Perhaps give her a rousing pep talk on waiting for the right guy to come along, with whom she could share the precious gift of her virginity.

It wasn't in his brief to take it—even if it had been offered to him. Virginity equalled vulnerability, and that equalled all sorts of unknown complications.

He had laid out the ground rules but she was a novice

to the game, so how was she supposed to know where he was coming from? She already thought him to be someone he wasn't. The situation was complicated enough as it stood, without her finding that she had got in over her head because of the sex.

He'd never had a problem jettisoning any of the women he had dated in the past. They had all been experienced, had all known the score. If some of them had been disappointed that they hadn't been able to convert him, then tough. All was fair in love and war.

His gut instinct told him that it would be different with Delilah if she turned sex into something it wasn't and would never be.

'You're not saying anything,' she muttered. 'I suppose you're horrified...'

Tears of humiliation sprang to her eyes and she gulped them back. She only had herself to blame. She had punched above her weight and this was where it had got her. It was to be expected. Any man who looked like a Greek god with a wealth of sexual experience behind him...any man who kicked off his affairs by telling the woman involved that he wasn't in it for the long term... was a man who would have no time for virgins.

'Not horrified...' Daniel corrected. 'Flattered. Turned on. Why would I be horrified?'

The more he thought about it, the more turned on he became. Her first... He physically ached to touch her, to show her just how fantastic sex could be... Even though the downside still continued to niggle away at the back of his mind...

He guided her hand to his bulging erection and grinned with a ridiculous surge of satisfaction as her eyes widened and her breathing hitched.

He was a big boy—a *very* big boy—and she was touching the evidence of just how turned on he was.

'But…' His voice was unsteady as he ploughed on with a conversation he knew he had to have. He'd had it before, but this time he had to make sure that she understood and accepted where he was coming from.

'But…?' Delilah whispered.

'You have no idea what you're doing to me right now,' he told her shakily.

He raked his fingers through his hair and shook his head, as though he might be able to clear it and regain some control over the situation. He'd never felt so out of control in his life before. It was as if he'd suddenly found himself stranded on foreign soil, with no landmarks to show him the direction he needed to take.

'Why me?' he asked flatly.

Delilah's breath hitched. 'If it's going to be a question-and-answer session about the fact that I didn't sleep with Michael, then I get the picture. I'm going to go now, and we can both pretend that this never happened. I told you I don't want to talk about it and I don't.'

She turned away. She'd had her reasons for keeping Michael at bay, even though she had supposedly been head over heels in love with him and planning their future, but she couldn't remember what they were now. Daniel's blunt incredulity made her decision to hold off sleeping with her ex feel freakish.

Daniel didn't answer. Instead he propelled her towards the bed and urged her down. Like a rag doll, she flopped onto it before sitting upright and drawing her knees to her chin, wrapping her arms around herself.

'It's not the most difficult question in the world to answer, Delilah.'

The dark, velvety tones of his voice washed over her soothingly, but she was still as tense as a bowstring and she huddled into herself as he, too, sat on the bed, though not within touching distance of her.

'I just don't see what that has to do with anything,' she told him mutinously.

'I'm not your Prince Charming,' Daniel said, without bothering to mince his words. Tough love. Or something like that. At any rate the laying of cards on the table, so that all misunderstandings could be avoided.

He was giving her a choice, and he couldn't be fairer than that, could he?

The mere fact that he was giving her a choice at all, when really he should be extricating himself from a possibly awkward situation in the making, was a little unnerving, but he fought down that unwelcome thought.

'Why would you think that you are?' Understanding dawned. 'Because I've chosen to sleep with you?' she said slowly. 'And you're so big-headed that you think the only reason I would do that is because I'm the sort of idiot who wants her fairytale ending to be with you…'

She swung her legs over the side of the bed before he could reach out to stop her and stood, shaking, arms tightly folded, staring at him and glaring.

'Of all the conceited, smug and, yes, *arrogant* men in the world, you just about have to take the biscuit!'

Taken aback by her anger, Daniel likewise vaulted upright, and they stood facing one another with the width of the bed separating them.

'What's a man supposed to think?' he demanded gruffly.

'Do you want to know *why* I chose to sleep with you?'

'You mean aside from the sizzling, irresistible attraction to me that you're powerless to fight…? The sort of sizzling, irresistible attraction you never felt for your loser ex…?'

Delilah blinked, because just like that the atmosphere between them had shifted.

Her whole body tightened and tensed, hyper-aware of

him, of his glorious masculine beauty, as he stood there, looking steadily at her, his thumbs hooked into the waistband of the trousers he hadn't got around to removing.

Antennae on red-hot alert, Daniel could almost feel something physical in the change in the air. Her eyes were still angry and accusing, but she was clutching herself just a little bit tighter, and her body was just a little bit more rigid—as though she had to use every ounce of willpower not to shatter into a thousand pieces.

'Did it never occur to you that you might be my adventure? The sort of adventure I need right now…at this point in time?' she flung at him.

He frowned. 'Explain.'

'Why should I? This was a big mistake…'

'Physical attraction is never a big mistake,' he said, in complete contradiction to what he had been thinking earlier.

Covering the small cabin in a couple of strides, he was looming over her before she had time to take evasive action. Not that her legs felt as though they could do any such thing. In fact, her legs were being very uncooperative at the moment, seemingly nailed to the floor, unable to move an inch, never mind take evasive action.

'Tell me what you meant when you said that I was your adventure.'

Delilah's heart was beating so fast and so hard that she could scarcely catch her breath, and she inhaled deeply in an attempt to establish some calm inside. Everywhere she looked her eyes ran slap-bang into something that set her nervous system hurtling towards meltdown.

Stare straight ahead and her vision was filled with the sight of his steel-hard, bronzed torso… Raise her eyes and she met his green, sexy ones… Look past him and what did she see? The bed. At which point the images that cluttered her head were enough to make her breathing go funny all over again.

'I went through something I thought was right, but it was only because I wanted it so badly to *be* right,' she whispered.

She found the safest point in the cabin and stared at it—it happened to be her feet. Not for long, though, because he raised her head so that she couldn't avoid looking at him.

'I felt like I'd spent my youth worrying about keeping the gallery afloat and worrying about Sarah working just to stand still. Michael was like a blast of fresh air, and it felt like he brought all sorts of exciting possibilities to my life. Maybe that was what I fell in love with. Maybe I was just desperate for a future that wasn't so...*predictable*. I'm only twenty-one, for heaven's sake! But it didn't work out, and I came here just to get away from...from everything. It was supposed to be just for a couple of weeks, but my art course proved so popular that I couldn't resist staying on—because when I return to the Cotswolds all I'm going to be doing is helping my sister in a last-ditch attempt to get the shop going, so that we have sufficient income to live on without having to worry about money all the time.'

Daniel had never had to worry about money. He and Theo had been born into privilege. Sure, his father had sent them both on their way to make their fortune, but they hadn't left the nest empty-handed. He had no doubt that both he and his brother would have succeeded whatever their backgrounds, because they both had the same drive, the same high-octane ambition that had fuelled their father and propelled him into making his fortune, but the fact remained that they had been born with silver spoons in their mouths.

Golden spoons, if he were to be perfectly honest.

He'd never delved into the details of any of his girl-friends' backgrounds, preferring to live in an uncluttered present which was mostly about sex, and of course the expensive fripperies that accompanied his very brief liaisons. Hearing about the sort of life Delilah was returning to brought into sharp relief the great big space between them.

It wasn't just the fact that she was green for her years, an innocent compared to his vastly more experienced self, but she was also, from the sound of it, broke.

Their worlds were so completely different that he might have been looking down at someone from another planet.

Under normal circumstances their paths would never have crossed, and yet now that they *had* crossed something about her had got to him and wasn't letting him go—wasn't allowing the voice of logic and reason to have a say.

'Have you ever been to the Cotswolds, Daniel?'

'I can't say that the countryside has ever done much for me...' he murmured.

'It's very beautiful. But very quiet. In winter, people hibernate. I love it there, but it's so quiet. It's a place where adventure would never happen to someone of my age.'

'You can't be the only young person there...'

'You'd be surprised how many of them move down to London to see a bit of the bright city lights before they return to the country to have kids and raise families.' She sighed. 'I wouldn't be able to do that because I have a duty to help Sarah, and that's something I want to do anyway, but...'

'But here you are, with one bad experience behind you—although from the sounds of it you don't need any sticking plaster—and here *I* am. And before you return to fulfil your sisterly obligations you don't see why you can't sleep with me on the rebound—have yourself a little fun and excitement before you take up your responsibilities with your sister... *I'm* your bright city lights before you return to the country...'

Did he like that? Daniel wasn't sure.

'That's more or less it.' She squashed the hint of defiance trying to creep into her voice. 'So if you think that I'm in any danger of falling for you, turning you into my Prince Charming, then you're way off track. That's not it at all. I've decided to...to... That you could be the one to...'

'To teach you the many and varying ways of enjoying love...?'

Delilah's mouth tightened, but her heart flipped at the slow smile playing on his lips.

The man was utterly incorrigible—and she had to admit, grudgingly, that that was just part and parcel of his overwhelming appeal.

'I may not be experienced,' she muttered, 'but that doesn't mean I don't have my head well and truly screwed on.'

'By which you mean...?'

Without her even realising he had taken her hand and led her back to the bed, and Delilah sank back against the pillows, not knowing whether she was relieved that this adventure was going to happen or terrified that this adventure was going to happen.

She was still fully clothed, her feet dangling off the bed, and before he joined her he knelt and removed her sandals, easing them off her feet in a gesture that was curiously delicate and erotic at the same time.

How odd that it was just the sort of thing a real-life Prince Charming might have done...

'...that I'm not the sort of catch you have in mind for yourself...?'

Daniel raised his eyes to hers and she shrugged and smiled and nodded all at the same time.

He was her adventure—someone she was prepared to have fun with, but certainly not the sort of man she would ever want as a permanent fixture in her life.

It couldn't be better. Could it? They were singing from the same song sheet and there was no way he should now be feeling as though his nose had been put out of joint by her admission.

'That's right,' she whispered.

She took a deep breath and held it, watching as he lowered his head to hers in slow motion. His kiss feathered her mouth, lingered, deepened, and at the same time he began removing her top. He cupped one small breast and then gently eased his hand underneath her stretchy bra. She shuddered against him.

'Feel good...?'

He breathed the question into her ear and Delilah gasped out a response, because now he was playing with her nipple and sending delicious shivers straight down from her breasts to the place between her legs which was growing wetter by the second.

'Want me...?' he asked. 'Because if I'm to be your rebound adventure, then I need to know that it's an adventure that you really want...'

'I want you, Daniel...' Her eyes fluttered open to meet his. He had the most amazing lashes. Dark and long and in striking contrast to his light hair.

'Good,' Daniel murmured with intense satisfaction. 'Now, I want you to relax. Don't worry. I'm not going to hurt you.'

Aren't you? she thought in sudden confusion. But the thought vanished as quickly as it had come and she settled back into the soft duvet with a sigh as he hoiked up the top, taking the bra with it so that her breasts were pushed free of the restricting fabric.

Her whole body shrieked in urgent response as he clamped his mouth over her nipple and began teasing it with his tongue, drawing it into his mouth, tasting the stiffened bud.

She had exquisite breasts. Small and neat, the nipples perfectly defined rosy-pink discs. Sexy breasts. Breasts a man could lose himself in.

Rampant desire was flooding through him, making him uncomfortable, making him wonder how the hell he was going to keep a lid on his natural urge to take her, fast and hard.

He straightened to pull her free of the top and the bra, and then for a few seconds stared down at her pale nudity, at the perfection of her slender body—the way the golden tan gave way to the paleness where her swimsuit had prevented the sun from touching her bare skin.

Her hair flowed over the pillow in an unruly mass and she had twisted her head to one side, squeezed her eyes shut, clenched her small fists at her sides.

He eased open her hands and she turned, opened her eyes, looked at him.

His erection was prominent against his trousers, pushing into a massive bulge that sent her senses spinning.

'Now we're both half naked,' he growled, 'shall we be really, really daring and go the whole way?'

Delilah smiled, and then nodded. Her natural instinct was to shield herself from his hungry gaze, but for some reason she wasn't feeling shy in front of him—something about the way he was looking at her…with blatant, open appreciation.

She wriggled sinuously and his nostrils flared. 'You

have no idea what you're doing to me,' he muttered in a wrenching undertone, and Delilah decided that she could happily cope with having that effect on him.

He vaulted upright and removed his trousers, and as he did so she propped herself up on one elbow and just... *stared*.

In fact, she found that she couldn't stop staring.

He removed his underwear, silky boxers, and she stilled. Although his erection had been visible underneath his trousers, now she could appreciate it in all its magnificent glory—and magnificent it really and truly was.

'I know I'm big...' He correctly interpreted her wide-eyed stare of apprehension. He perched on the side of the bed and grinned. 'But I won't hurt you. Promise. I'll be very, very gentle, and in the end you'll be begging me to go harder...'

He began easing off her silky trousers, tugging them down until she was left in just her underwear. Simple cotton pants that made him smile, because they was a world apart from the lacy lingerie women always but *always* wore for him.

But then there wasn't a single bone in her body that advertised herself, was there?

Underneath her clothes she was as unaffected as she was everywhere else, and he liked that. A lot.

He didn't immediately tug down her underwear, even though she was squirming, her own hands reaching to do the job for him. Instead he pressed the flat of his hand between her legs, feeling the dampness spreading through the cotton, and firmly began to massage her, knowing just where to apply pressure so that her squirming was now accompanied by soft groans and whimpers.

He didn't stop. He wanted her on the brink of tipping over the edge. He wanted her so wet for him that he would slide into her, and she would stretch and take all of him, and love every second of the experience.

He was going to make sure that nothing hurt.

Even if he had to dig deep to find the self-restraint he would need.

'Please, Daniel…' His hand down there was sweet, sweet torture. Her body was on fire and he just kept on rubbing, until she thought she was going out of her mind. 'If you don't stop…'

'If I don't stop what…? You'll come against my hand?'

'You know I will,' she panted. 'And I don't want it to be like this… It should…should…'

'There are no *shoulds* when it comes to making love,' Daniel admonished teasingly. 'It's all about what makes you feel good. Does this feel good?'

'Better than good…'

She could barely get the words out, and when he slipped that questing hand under her panties, so that he was rubbing her properly, finding the throbbing bud of her clitoris and teasing it remorselessly, she wanted to faint.

She spread apart her legs and her body found its own rhythm as she began to move, angling herself so that he could slip one finger, then two, into her, while making sure to keep pressure on her clitoris. Straining under the bombardment of sensation, unable to hold off any longer, even though she wanted to, Delilah tensed, arched, and with a keening cry came against his fingers.

It was beautiful, he thought, dazed at the ferocity of his reaction to seeing her reach orgasm. Colour flooded her cheeks and she was breathing fast and shallow, and as she raised her body off the bed he thrust his fingers deeper into her, extending her orgasm and deepening it. Her face was shiny with perspiration.

If he could stop himself from ejaculating like a bloody

horny teenager, then he could do anything, he figured—because right now that felt like the hardest thing in the world to achieve.

'It shouldn't have been like that.' Delilah was dismayed, because this was just more evidence of her inexperience, but he was smiling as he lowered himself alongside her.

'Shh…'

'But I want to…to give you pleasure as well…'

'You are.'

'Tell me what to do.'

'You can hold me,' he suggested. 'But just hold me,' he warned. 'Because I might come if you do much more. I'm *that* close to losing control…'

'I bet you never do.'

'Lose control? Never. You, however, are turning out to be the exception to the rule when it comes to getting me to that point. Now, I'm going to touch you everywhere… with my mouth…with my hands…very, very slowly. I just want you to enjoy the experience, Delilah, and stop thinking that there should be a certain way of doing things…'

'Is that an order?' she whispered. She raised herself up to plant feathery kisses all over his face, ending with his beautiful mouth, but that was as far as he would allow her to go.

Masterful.

That was the word that sprang to mind, and his mastery thrilled her to her very core.

He kissed her neck and then spent time on her breasts, giving her body time to subside from its orgasm, time to find its way to building back up to a new peak. He kissed her flat stomach and felt her suck in her breath, then trailed lower, gently parting her legs to accommodate him.

He settled himself between her legs and then rested

them over his shoulders, and then he kissed and licked and teased her in her most intimate spot—and she loved every second of it. She gave herself to his exploration with an abandonment she would never have believed possible. His tongue flicked over her clitoris and she stiffened as she began to melt.

But this time he didn't let her build up the momentum that would take her over the edge. Instead, he teased her. He aroused her. He took her so far and then away, so that she had time to catch her breath, and the more he did that, the more she pleaded with him to come into her.

And in the end he just had to—because he was losing too much of his self-control to do anything else…

His wallet was on the ground and he barely looked as he flipped a condom over his rock-hard erection.

She was tight and wet and he eased himself inside her gently, in a two steps forward, one step back process that gradually allowed her to relax, so that he could fit into her without her tensing.

When he was ready to sink deeper into her, to have his shaft fill her, so was she, and as he thrust in, pushing her up the bed, taking his time and being as gentle as he could, he heard and felt the long, low shudder of her reaching orgasm.

It took her over.

Delilah hadn't thought that this depth of pure, unfiltered sensation could even exist. It did. She had stretched for him and moulded around his bigness as though their bodies had been made for one another. She came over and over and over, just as he reared up, the tendons in his neck straining, and came into her.

Time stood still. When finally they were back on Planet Earth she curved into him with a sigh of pure contentment. 'That was… Thank you…'

The disarming charm of her words distracted him from

the pressing concern that his condom appeared to have split. He chucked it onto the pile of clothes on the ground and wrapped his arms around her, drew her against him.

Mind-blowing. That was the only way he could describe the experience. Had it been because of the situation? Because she'd come to him a virgin? Or had it been because she had no idea of his identity? No idea of who he really was and how much he was really worth?

For just the briefest of moments he was disconcerted by that—by the very thing that had turned him on: namely her ignorance of his monetary value. He was disconcerted by the fact that she didn't know the truth about him.

'There's no need to thank me,' he told her huskily. He pushed back some wayward strands of hair. 'But there's something just a little bit worrying I have to say...'

'What's that?'

'I think the condom may have split...is that a problem? By which I mean are you in a safe period? It's highly unlikely that anything unfortunate will happen, but I thought I'd mention it...'

Delilah thought quickly and decided that she was perfectly safe, even though there *had* been a little hiccup—what with the travel and the stress and the sheer excitement of being on the cruise liner.

'Perfectly safe,' she told him firmly, nestling into him and smiling as she felt him stir against her naked thighs.

Daniel couldn't credit that his body was already gearing up for a repeat performance—one which it would not have...not just yet...because chances were that she would be sore.

The surprising urgency of his response settled his mind on the very pleasant prospect of what remained of the rest of his incognito holiday aboard the liner.

'Good,' he murmured, although he was already thinking ahead, wanting her in ways he couldn't remember wanting any other woman for a very long time. 'Glad to hear it.'

Delilah didn't add the reassurance that it was rare for a woman to fall pregnant on her first sexual encounter. She had read enough magazines to know that that was a myth.

'Now, how do you think we should spend the rest of the evening?' he asked.

She giggled and moved against him, and he grinned.

'Your body will need to take a little rest. I'd suggest we share a shower, but the facilities here leave a lot to be desired when it comes to joint showers... All cabins should cater for couples who want to have sex in the bathroom, don't you agree?'

'I don't think I've ever been in a shower that can fit more than one very skinny person.' She couldn't stop herself from touching him. She touched his hair, stroked his cheek, drew over the fine lines at the corners of his eyes with her fingers...

Daniel thought of the vast bathroom at his house in Sydney. The vast bathrooms at all the places he owned. He liked big bathrooms. Small, cosy spaces didn't do it for him.

What would she think if she knew the truth about him?

Just like that the question sprang from nowhere, and he frowned. She'd turn into just someone else who was desperate to please him, he decided, which was why it was refreshing that she didn't know.

'One shower at a time,' he said, with audible regret in his voice. 'Then what about you telling me about *my* half of this deal...?'

'Deal?' Delilah looked at him, perplexed, and he burst out laughing.

'I like the compliment,' he said with satisfaction. 'You've forgotten that, in return for me getting my wicked and very, very enjoyable way with you, you get to paint me... Talk to me about that. You can even put me in whatever sexy pose you want, and I guarantee that by the time we're finished talking about that we'll both be ready to make love all over again...'

CHAPTER SIX

'IT LOOKS GOOD...' Lying on his bed, arms folded behind his head, Daniel looked at the half-finished portrait of himself.

Somehow Delilah had managed to squeeze an easel into a corner of the cabin, so that she could paint him without being observed by all and sundry.

Daniel thought that had been an inspired idea, considering the portrait of him showed him in the position he was in now—reclining half naked on the bed, with a swirl of duvet blatantly advertising the fact that underneath it he was wearing nothing at all.

'You're not supposed to talk.'

But she smiled, because they did a lot of talking while he was posing for her and she liked that. They didn't talk about anything in particular. The conversation ebbed and flowed, drifted in and out of topics, and although there were vast swathes of his life which she felt she knew precious little about, she still felt that she knew the whole man, the complete package—knew the things that made him laugh and the things that pissed him off.

For three hours every day, for a week and a half now, he had been her captive audience, and it had bred an easy familiarity between them that thrilled her to the bone. If this was what successful therapy was all about then she was a fervent fan, because she hadn't thought about

Michael once, and she hadn't thought about the gallery either.

And she still hadn't tired of just *looking* at him. She knew every angle of his face and every muscle and sinew of his beautiful, strong body.

'It's utterly boring, trying to maintain this pose, if I can't talk at the same time.'

Or work. Or make the important business calls that needed to be made. Or do any of the other things around which his life was normally focused.

The truth was that he had shoved work commitments to one side, only really catching up after she had left him late in the night to return to her cabin. It was a fairly hellish routine when it came to grabbing much sleep, but frankly he didn't care. He was having a good time, and he saw no reason why he shouldn't indulge himself a little. The world wasn't going to stop turning on its axis just because he didn't clock in for a conference call at a prearranged time, or because he delegated a call to one of his guys at Head Office.

He was enjoying her.

And after that first time, when nerves had almost got the better of her, she had opened up to him like a peach.

His eyes flared now as he watched her painting him, her expression one of ferocious concentration.

That ferocious concentration was somewhat diluted by the fact that she wore nothing as she sat at her easel painting him. That was part of *his* side of the deal—a little addendum he had tacked on, and one which she had agreed to without, it had to be said, much persuasion.

She had a glorious body. Having previously only gone for women who were curvy and big-breasted, like pocket-sized Barbie dolls, he found that he couldn't get enough of her slender length, her long, shapely legs, her colt-like grace, the sweep of her hair…

Jarring at the back of his mind was the thought that all too soon it would have to come to an end. He'd already outstayed his original allotted time. He'd visited two countries more than he'd planned on doing. He'd produced more laughable attempts at still-life painting than any man should ever have to do. And he'd had the most mind-blowing sex…

Every day. Every night. More than once a night.

Just thinking about that mind-blowing sex was making him harden, and he knew that very shortly he would have to have her.

Delilah could sense where his thoughts were going without even having to look at the darkening in his eyes. It was as if they were connected by some kind of invisible umbilical cord to one another. He wanted her. And she wanted him.

Her nipples pinched at the thought of it and she wasn't shocked when he levered himself off the bed and strolled towards her.

Their routine of painting took place after lunch, when her classes were over. A lazy time for both of them. The sun continued to shine outside and the deep blue ocean continued to spread around them like a never-ending swathe of navy blue silk, but the only thing she had room for in her head was *him*.

He occupied every waking moment of her thoughts and most of her sleeping ones, as well.

'This portrait will never get finished if you keep interrupting me like this…' She looked up at him and grinned, her body already gearing up to unite with his, liquid pooling between her legs in anticipation.

Her breath hitched as he touched himself, touched his big, hard erection.

'My muscles were seizing up,' he drawled. 'I'm a man who enjoys lots of exercise. Physical activity.'

'I can point you in the direction of the squash courts,' she suggested helpfully. 'They could do with a lick of paint, but they function fine, and I'm sure you could rustle up a suitable partner if you want to get some much needed exercise...'

'I have a feeling that the way I play might spell certain death for whoever happens to be playing against me. Some of the guys here look as though they may have dodgy tickers...'

Delilah laughed, on a breathless high. So much for getting that bit of his arm just right... She could barely concentrate when he was posing for her, and when he was standing in front of her as he was doing now, butt naked and aroused, it was impossible.

She swivelled on the chair so that she was facing him, and then she stood on her tiptoes and kissed him—a lingering kiss that was as sweet and seductive as honey.

You thrill me, she would have liked to have told him, but that was off-limits. She knew that without having to be told. That sort of thing was taboo. Words of endearment or any hint at all that this might be deeper and more significant than either of them had bargained for were never spoken.

It wasn't love—of course it wasn't—but it *felt* as if it should be more than just a two-week fling...

When she thought about him disappearing she felt physically sick, so she tried not to think about it.

Instead, she thought about the fact that he had already stayed on for longer than he had first said he would, and she couldn't help pathetically wondering what that meant.

'Nice...' Daniel murmured, smiling down at her. 'Much better than lying on a bed pretending to be a statue.'

'You make a terrible model.'

'And here I was thinking that you found me good-looking...'

'Lord, but you're conceited. And that's not what I meant. You're far too restless to make a good model. Even when you're trying to stay perfectly still I can *hear* your brain whirring and I know you're itching to get up…'

'How well you know me, my little artist. Now, shall we put that to the test?'

'Put what to the test?'

'Your knowledge of me… Tell me what I'm thinking I'd like you to do now…'

Afterwards, lying on his bed, both on their backs, with her head resting on his shoulder, the pressing question of his imminent departure again began playing on his mind.

This wasn't going to do.

He couldn't play truant from reality for ever, and that was what he'd been doing. Good fun, but the time to say goodbye had come.

Conference calls had been cancelled, delegated, post-poned…in one instance flatly avoided…but the final grain of sand had sifted through the upturned egg timer and now he had to leave.

A new acquisition required his urgent attention, and decisions had to be made about an office block he intended to refurbish in Mayfair. He couldn't duck low for ever.

However sweet the temptation was.

He turned to the sweet temptation and stroked her breast, looking down and smiling with male appreciation at the way her nipple tightened under the brush of his finger.

Propping himself up on his elbow, he continued to feather his finger over the stiffened pink bud before lowering his head to tease it with his tongue, then his mouth, suckling on it, but not touching her anywhere else at all.

Driving her crazy with just his mouth clamped to her nipple.

She squirmed and fidgeted, her whole body yearning for his—a physical ache that needed to be sated.

She'd learned how to touch him, where to touch him, the places that turned him on, and she reached down to close her hand over his erection, moving it slowly but firmly, building a little pace until she could tell from the change in his breathing that he was as turned on as she was.

And this, Daniel thought, was how things had ended up where they had—how he had ended up staying far longer than he had anticipated or planned.

This senseless drive to have more and more of her.

He laid his hand over hers and gritted his teeth, willing his erection to subside, because he couldn't think straight when he was aroused. It was as if she took over his whole mind.

After a couple of minutes he flipped onto his back and stared for a few seconds at the ceiling of the cabin.

If he looked through the circular window he would see the clear turquoise sky and the sun shining down on the navy blue ocean. When he took to the water in Australia he sailed with purpose, pitting his skill against nature. He got up close and personal with the sea, felt the whip of breeze on his face, challenged the ocean's depths to do their worst.

It was nothing like this. He thought that perhaps this was what people meant when they said that they'd had a 'relaxing' holiday. This was what doing nothing was all about, and he realised that it was something he rarely did. He hadn't even suspected how enjoyable it could be.

'We need to talk.'

In one easy, fluid movement Daniel slipped out of bed

and stood by the side for a few seconds, looking at her flushed face, at the flare of dismay in her eyes.

Was he going to tell her everything?

When they'd started their fling he'd presumed that he would leave the ship, wave goodbye and she would never be any the wiser as to his true identity. A few hot nights of passion and then a parting of ways.

He would conduct his business transaction with the Ockleys either from London or Sydney. He'd got the information he needed about the liner, had seen for himself what the crew were like. He even had his offer formulated in his head. It was low, but then the liner was fairly run down and would hit the metaphorical rocks within the next year or so. It was an offer he knew they might resent, but would be compelled to accept. In his eyes, that amounted to what was *fair*.

He hadn't planned on staying for as long as he had.

He hadn't planned on a number of things.

He frowned and had a quick mental flashback of her laughing, head thrown back…her concentration in her art classes, patiently giving encouragement to everyone… her blushing and laughing whenever he touched her or whenever she touched him…

'You might want to get dressed…'

He knew that this was for his benefit rather than hers. He couldn't think straight when she was naked, and he needed to think straight. This was just another woman he was going to leave behind, and he tightened his jaw in preparation for his parting speech.

Delilah sprang out of the bed. Her heart was beating so hard that it felt as though it might explode right out of her chest.

It was going to end.

He'd never promised otherwise. Had never hinted at it. Now, however, she realised just how much she had hoped that there might be a future for them. She'd somehow become needy and clingy and it appalled her.

What had happened to all her grand theories about the nature of lust? What had happened to her conviction that she couldn't be hurt if she slept with him because you could only be hurt when you were in love? What had happened to her assumption that love could never enter the equation because he was just a bit of fun to take her mind off the bad time she'd had with Michael and the worrying time that lay ahead with all their money problems?

Thoughts swarming in her head like angry bees, she fought against the realisation that she had fallen in love with him.

With beautiful, intelligent, utterly charismatic Daniel —who was a commitment-phobe, who didn't want to put down roots, who was just taking a breather with her in between his travels…

Just by being himself he had made her see how shallow Michael had been and how unsuitable as a partner.

She dressed quickly, barely able to look at him, already bracing herself for his 'Dear John' speech.

And the worst of it was that she wanted to beg him not to deliver the speech—wanted to tell him that they worked so well together, that they should try and continue what they had…that they had something special.

Except it was only special *for her*, wasn't it…?

'I know what you're going to say.'

'Do you?'

He didn't think so.

'You're going to tell me that you're moving on…that you have places to go, people to see…' She gave a brittle laugh and stared at him, chin tilted at a defiant angle.

Daniel thought that he might miss those shapeless long skirts and baggy tops.

'I never led you to believe that this would be a permanent arrangement.' He shoved his hands into his trouser pockets and then ran his fingers through his hair. He wanted to walk…to burn off some of his restless energy… but the cabin was the size of a matchbox so he settled for dragging the chair from the fitted dressing table by the wall and sitting down heavily.

'I know,' Delilah said tightly.

She badly wanted to beg him to reconsider. Her hands were shaking and she pushed them into the deep pockets of her skirt and perched on the edge of the bed.

'I don't do long-term,' he told her in the sort of gentle voice that set her teeth on edge. 'And there's a reason for that.'

'You've had your heart broken.'

'I've had my heart *hardened*.' He sighed. 'What do you think of this cruise liner?'

'Sorry?' She raised startled eyes to his and wondered where this was going. Was that *it* for his goodbye speech? Didn't she deserve more? Maybe just a tiny bit of remorse?

'What do you think of this cruise liner? I mean the way it's run…its condition…the general state of its health?'

'I… Well… I don't know where you're going with this, Daniel.' When he didn't answer, she gave a little shrug and looked around her. 'It could do with some work,' she said, still bewildered. 'Everyone knows that. All the crew know that Gerry and Christine have been having a few financial problems…'

'They're heavily in debt. Your eyes would water if you knew how much they owed the bank. They inherited this liner from Gerry's parents. A very wealthy family, as it happens. Lots of fingers in lots of pies. This was just one of their concerns. Unfortunately Gerry Ockley may have inherited their wealth—which, frankly, was already dwindling by the time John Ockley kicked the bucket—

but he has failed to inherit his father's business acumen. The estate was evenly divided between three sons and he got the liner as part of his legacy. He turned a niche and nicely profitable service into something equally niche but sadly not nearly as profitable.'

Her mouth had dropped open. He knew every single illusion she had had about him was slowly being shattered, but he had to continue, and he told himself that shattered illusions weren't such a bad thing.

He'd grown from his, hadn't he? Shattered illusions allowed you to develop the sort of tough strength that helped you get through life. That was how it had worked for him. She would move on from this a much stronger person.

He banked down the tide of savage guilt that *he* was the one responsible for giving her this learning curve.

'I am Daniel De Angelis,' he told her softly. 'You think that I'm a traveller, interested in dabbling in a spot of art, but that's not strictly speaking the truth…'

'I don't know what you're telling me…' Delilah shook her head in utter bewilderment. She felt as though she had suddenly been transported into a parallel universe, where everything looked the same but nothing actually was.

Her warm, teasing, sexy guy had vanished and in his place was this stranger, with his remote, guarded eyes, saying stuff that she didn't understand.

'I didn't come here to do a course on art,' he ploughed on—relentless, remorseless.

She wished she could just put her hand over his beautiful mouth and stop the flow of words.

'I came here to inspect this liner…to find out where its failings lay…to see its condition first-hand and to do it without anyone knowing who I was… I wanted the element of surprise—no superficial tidying or paint jobs. I wanted to see it in all its downtrodden glory…'

'But *why*?' Delilah whispered, her voice barely audible.

'Because I intend to buy it.'

That flatly spoken statement swirled around her like thick toxic waste, penetrating her consciousness, and then she was tying up all the things that hadn't made sense about him—starting with that ridiculously extravagant dinner on the deck…their first *date*. What a joke!

Anger began a slow, poisonous burn.

'You're not poor at all, are you?' She knew that she was stating the obvious, but there was still a pathetic part of her that was clinging to the hope that this was all some kind of big joke.

'I am a billionaire,' Daniel said.

No beating around the bush. He looked for the signs he secretly expected to see. The flare of certain interest as her preconceived notions gave way to far more tempting prospects.

They failed to materialise.

And along with that realisation came another one.

He wasn't ready to let her go. Not yet. Eventually, yes. But not yet. He still wanted her.

So now she would know the truth about him—but the bottom line was that he was very, very, *very* rich, and that, in the end, would be the deciding factor.

Women were always predictable in their reactions to extreme wealth. They gravitated towards it like bears to a pot of honey. Once she'd recovered from the shock of his revelations she would surely see the advantages of continuing what they had—not least because it was what she wanted.

He still desired her, and she still desired him—it was simple as that when you cut through all the murky red tape.

Goodbye speeches weren't set in cement, were they? And he didn't want to walk away leaving behind unfinished business. He didn't want to find himself missing those long, shapeless skirts and baggy tops and wondering whether he should have continued what they had.

Practical to the very last drop of blood in his body, Daniel knew that the fact that she was broke would work in his favour. He wondered whether she would be insulted if he offered to help her and her sister out of their dire financial situation...

'Why did you get involved with me?' Delilah asked bluntly. She had to clench her fists to stop her hands from shaking uncontrollably. Like a jigsaw puzzle, the pieces were all coming together, thick and fast, and what she was beginning to see of the finished picture made her feel sick.

'I didn't intend to get involved with *anyone*,' Daniel told her truthfully.

'But here I was and so you decided *why not*? Because I guess you're the kind of guy who always takes what he wants, and I'm thinking that you maybe decided you could kill two birds with one stone. You wanted all sorts of information about the ship and the people who worked on it, and you decided that I might be able to help you out with some of that information.'

Her voice was rising, even though she was trying to keep it calm and controlled. She just knew that if she really let what he had just told her overwhelm her then she would fly at him, and she wasn't going to do that. She was going to walk away and leave him with the contempt he deserved.

But underneath it all she could feel her heart breaking in two.

She'd been the biggest idiot in the world. She'd wanted adventure and she'd got a hell of a lot more than she'd bargained for. She'd got a nightmare.

She should have listened to her sister and to her own common sense. You couldn't clear your head of one stupid mistake with a guy by jumping into bed the second someone else came around.

Daniel flushed darkly. Strictly speaking, there was an element of truth there... But hadn't events put a different spin on it? Things had changed. But he couldn't deny that he *had* seen her as a good conduit of information for him and now, thinking about that, he was prey to a certain amount of guilt.

'You lied to me all along,' she said tautly. 'You lied about who you were, and you lied about what you wanted from me... The only thing you said to me that was true was that you weren't going to be sticking around and that you weren't interested in long-lasting relationships... Aside from that, every single thing you said to me was a lie. All lies!'

'I didn't lie to you about wanting you.'

His husky voice penetrated her anger and she hated herself for the way her body weakened. Even hating him, he could still do that—still make her insides go to mush— and she hated him even more for being able to do that.

Keep it cold, and hang on to your self-control...

'So what do you intend to do now?' she demanded. 'Throw everyone overboard and take over the liner? Like some kind of pirate?'

He *looked* like a pirate. She should have listened to her instincts and followed them... Should have realised early on that he just didn't fit the profile of an itinerant traveller, aimlessly seeing the world and stopping off to indulge his love of art.

No wonder his efforts at drawing and painting had been so poorly executed. In fact little wonder that he had barely put paint to canvas in all the classes he had so dutifully attended.

'I'm not the bad guy here,' Daniel told her, outraged

at the attacks being levelled against him, even though he could understand some of her justifiable fury.

Hell, if she looked at the bigger picture she would see that he would be doing the hapless Ockleys a favour by buying them out!

'Oh, you're an absolute saint.' Delilah's voice dripped sarcasm.

'The Ockleys are going under,' Daniel informed her, even though he was distracted by her glorious beauty—all rage and tousled hair and pursed lips. 'They're on a fast track to bankruptcy and when that happens they'll get nothing for this ship. It'll be taken off their hands for a song. I intend to buy it and bring it back up to spec…'

'And you think that I'm supposed to *congratulate* you for that? You *used* me.'

'You're overreacting.'

Delilah resisted the strong temptation to throw something at him. His stupid portrait would do the trick.

But even as she thought that another treacherous thought crossed her mind.

That portrait would be all she had left of him when they parted ways. And she hated herself for wanting to hang on to it.

'So what happens to all the people who depend on this liner for their livelihoods?' she flung at him, slamming the door on her weakness.

'I'm not going to throw them overboard!' Daniel thundered. 'You're being dramatic! I… Okay, so I apologise if you think that you were used…' Dull colour highlighted his cheekbones. Apologies were something else he didn't do. 'I intend to keep the staff who are up to the job. They'll find that they're richly rewarded and working on a ship that's actually not hanging on to survival by the skin of its pants!'

'I hate you.'

'You don't hate me,' he said huskily. 'You want me. If I came over there right now and kissed you, you'd kiss me back and you'd want more…'

'You wouldn't dare…' She glared at him.

'You should know better than to lay down challenges like that to a man like me.'

The air was charged as they stared at one another in electric silence.

'I should have seen the signs,' she muttered. 'I should have known from the very first moment you had that meal arranged on deck and paid poor Stan extra money that you weren't who you said you were!'

'*Poor Stan* will be singing my praises when I tell him what sort of money he'll be getting when he works for *me*.'

'And I suppose you'll turn this ship into some awful, rowdy, drink-all-you-can cruiser for the under-thirties…?' she said scathingly.

'The opposite—'

'And all that rubbish you told me about not being the sort of guy who wants long-term relationships… I suppose you were just referring to *me*…' Hurt and bitterness had crept into her voice as she dispassionately joined up all the dots. 'You're just an opportunist who decided to take advantage of a vulnerable woman. And you knew I was vulnerable… You knew I'd just come out of a bad relationship—that I wasn't looking forward to going back to the Cotswolds and facing all those financial problems…'

Considering he had spent his life making sure to avoid opportunists, Daniel was enraged that she had flung him into that category.

'I don't *do* relationships,' he told her flatly. 'Nothing to do with you. And I didn't drag you kicking and screaming against your will into the nearest bed because you were *vulnerable*!'

'But you knew that I *was*!'

'I didn't take you for a coward, Delilah.'

'What does *that* mean?'

'Face up to the choices you made. You knew what you were getting into. You knew I wasn't in it for the long haul. You *chose* to sleep with me. That was the decision *you* made—and, trust me, if you'd decided against it I would never have tried to force your hand. So do me a favour and take responsibility for your decisions!'

'I just never thought that I was going to end up in bed with a liar! I thought I'd been there, done that. I thought you were *different*.'

Daniel's teeth snapped, but there was nothing he could say to that.

'And if you *were* to "do" a relationship,' Delilah inserted in a driven voice, 'then it certainly wouldn't be with someone like *me,* would it? Someone without money? Not when you're a billionaire who can buy a cruise ship the way someone might buy a pair of shoes!'

His silence was telling.

'I'm careful,' he gritted. 'I'm a target for gold-diggers. That's just the way it is.'

'I think I've heard enough now,' Delilah said quietly. She felt utterly drained, exhausted on every level. Her legs were like jelly and she hoped that when she stood up she wouldn't go crashing to the ground. 'I'm going to take my painting with me, if you don't mind.'

She began easing the canvas from the easel, her back to him, not looking at him, although she was aware of his presence with every atom of her body.

If he touched her now...

She knew that she had to get out of the cabin as fast as she could—because she didn't trust herself...didn't know what she would do if he touched her now...and the last thing she wanted was to give him any excuse for thinking that she was the kind of mug who was so smitten with him that she would melt in his arms like the fool she'd been.

No way.

'This doesn't have to end here,' Daniel said gruffly.

She spun round to look at him with an expression of scorn.

He *never* pursued a woman. And especially in a situation like this, when he was staring at a woman who wanted no more to do with him… Pursuit should *definitely* be off the agenda. But, hell, he still wanted her, and he was driven by his own physical impulse.

'I still want you,' he told her.

'So you said. But we can't always have what we want.'

'You have no idea what I could give you.'

'A brief fling?' she enquired with saccharine sweetness. 'A couple more weeks until you get tired of me?'

'You could have anything you want,' he intoned, shocked that he was going down this road. 'You say that you and your sister are short of cash? Struggling to make ends meet? I could help you with that. I could inject money into your business, pull out all the stops, get it to a place where you'd never have to worry about money again…'

Considering her sister didn't know a thing about Daniel,—thank heavens—Delilah wondered what she would think if she brought him home and produced him as their knight in shining armour.

What a laugh.

As if he could *ever* be her knight in shining armour.

And 'pull out all the stops'? Rescue them from their financial situation? How long before he started thinking that she was just another one of those gold-diggers who saw him as a target?

She walked towards the door and said cuttingly, 'I don't think so. I don't want you *or* your money. I'd appreciate it if you just left me alone for the remainder of your time on this liner. I don't want you to come to my classes, and if you see me in the bar or the restaurant feel free to ignore me.'

She couldn't believe that her voice was as cool and controlled as it was, when inside she was falling apart at the seams.

Sex.

That was what she meant to him and that was *all* she meant to him. He still wanted her, and he didn't see why his lies and deception should stand in the way of getting what he wanted—especially when he could throw his money into the ring and try and tempt her with it. Try and *buy* her with it.

Daniel looked at her frozen expression. He had been locked out and he wasn't going to beg.

'And what do you think your students and your fellow crew members are going to think?' he asked. 'Unless they're blind, they already know that there's something going on between us…'

Delilah hitched her shoulder in a dismissive shrug. 'Like you told me at the very beginning—who cares? Why should I care what other people think when I won't be seeing any of them again?'

She wondered how much longer he would stay on the liner and thought that it wouldn't be long. Off at the next stop, having pulled the plug on Christine and Gerry. When she left this cabin she wouldn't be seeing him again. She would make sure of that, however hard it might be.

She didn't look back at him as she let herself out of the cabin. She walked quickly—away from people, away from the possibility of anyone seeing her and guessing that something was wrong. She didn't want to bump into any of her students or any of the other crew members… didn't want them to ask her if she was okay.

She just wanted to get back to the safety of her own cramped cabin and give in to the tears that she was struggling to hold back.

She just wanted to go home.

CHAPTER SEVEN

DELILAH GAZED UP at the building in front of her. It wasn't one of those vast, impressive glass houses that broadcasted to the world that the worker bees inside were *very important* worker bees. By comparison this was a modest building, just three storeys high, a squat, square and rather old-fashioned red brick affair, away from the chaotic hustle and bustle of the city.

She didn't want to be here, but she had had to jump through hoops to find the wretched place and now that she was standing in front of it she wasn't going to retreat without seeing him.

Which didn't mean that she wasn't as nervous as a kitten.

In a sudden burst of anxiety she spun away from the building and headed to the nearest coffee shop, where she would try and rally her mental troops.

The heat of the Mediterranean sun seemed like a long, long time ago. Much longer than two months, which was when she had said farewell to the liner and to the friends she had made there.

Everything had been so chaotic.

Like a hurricane, Daniel had swept through them all and changed their lives in one way or another.

For Christine and Gerry, after what she had privately admitted must have been a horrible, horrible shock to the system, because they had both viewed the money he had flung down on the table as a hostile takeover, things had actually turned out okay.

Faced with the brutal facts of their financial situation, they had been forced to get their heads out of the sand and abandon their optimism that the tide was going to change—that they just needed a couple of bumper seasons, that hordes of culture vultures were waiting out there to book passages on their once-in-a-lifetime cruise.

And, Gerry had told her, Daniel's offer had been pretty fair—which had somewhat eroded Delilah's assumption that Daniel's sole interest had been to plunder and take for the cheapest possible price.

Which, of course, didn't excuse the fact that he had used her and lied to her.

Most the crew were to be re-employed, back on the liner, with six months of paid leave while the cruise ship was being renovated, and their salaries were now so inflated that they were overjoyed at the change of ownership. Stan, as Daniel had told her, had been over the moon at the prospect of running his own kitchen, no expense spared.

The other tutors had thought nothing of losing their jobs. Some, like her, had been part-time recruits and the rest, all in their mid-fifties, had been happy enough to use their talents in other directions. The liner had not constituted their sole income.

No one had been left with the corrosive bitterness that she had been left with—but then she had been in a unique situation.

As predicted, she had seen nothing of him, and had no idea how long he'd remained on the liner before leaving. She had hidden away, taking meals in her poky cabin and scuttling to her classes in a state of dread that she might see him sprawled in his usual chair, doing something and nothing in front of his easel.

He had not reappeared.

So much for his heated pursuit. So much for all that rubbish about still wanting her. He had given it one shot and then shrugged his shoulders and walked away. Literally jumped ship.

Delilah had told herself that she was hugely relieved, but somewhere deep inside disappointment had gnawed away at her, making her situation even more awful and painful than it already had been.

Everything had dissolved. There had been tearful goodbyes and promises to keep in touch. Many of the students had expressed an interest in the business she and Sarah would be starting, which was something, at least.

She had put a brave smile on her face. Several people had asked her about Daniel, asked her whether she would be seeing him again, and she had laughed and told them that it had been nothing more than a pleasant holiday fling.

All lies.

She had fallen in love and was she ever going to recover? Was there a Mr Right? A Mr Sensible and Suited To Her? The sort of chap she should have been looking for after Michael, who was going to elbow Mr Utterly Wrong out of the spot in her heart which he continued to occupy?

Even after everything had gone quiet.

Even after she'd returned to the Cotswolds.

After she'd done her very best to clear her head of him.

She still missed him. She missed him so much that she had gone through all the motions of helping Sarah and enthusing about their project like an automaton.

She missed him so much that she hadn't paid a scrap of attention to the fact that she had skipped a period, and it had only been when she'd started feeling sick and nauseous at certain smells and when certain foods were presented to her that she had twigged.

She closed her eyes briefly and relived that moment when time had stood still. Two bright blue lines had marked the end of life as she knew it. She could still taste the fear, the panic, and see the blank fog of confusion that had crashed over her like a tsunami. Then, when the utter shock had subsided, had come the numbness of just not knowing what happened next.

She opened her eyes and through the window of the coffee shop watched the crowds outside, scurrying about their business.

She had managed to find out, from Christine, where he was and how long he would be there. They, of course, were in touch with him, finalising the sale of their liner.

'He's not the predator we first thought,' Christine had confided. 'And his plans for the liner sound really interesting. Nothing we could ever have hoped to do in a million years… Literally catering for the rich and famous—and would you believe he's actually told me and Gerry that we can have three weeks a year free cruising for the rest of our lives? A way of keeping in touch with our beloved *Rambling Rose*. He didn't have to do that…'

Delilah's brain had stopped functioning at the word *predator*. That was what he was. A predator. He had obviously charmed Gerry and Christine, but she had no doubt that he would have done a pretty shrewd deal and then wrapped it up in lots of glitzy packaging so that he came out of it smelling of roses.

They might have been charmed.

They might have ended up thinking that he'd been a real sport and given them a good deal.

But *she* knew better than to judge a book by its cover. He was one of life's takers. She felt that he could have told her at *any time* who he really was. But he hadn't. Hadn't even come close. He'd been perfectly happy to string her along and she knew why.

At the end of the day there was no way that he would ever allow himself to become involved with someone he considered his inferior.

He played around with women, but in the end they were all potential gold-diggers and therefore only worthy of short-term meaningless dalliances.

Of which she had been one. One of a long number. He'd practically said so himself.

Unfortunately, even with that perfectly sound reasoning, she had still spent weeks thinking obsessively about him. She'd resisted telling her sister about her escapade, because she hadn't wanted any I-told-you-so lectures, but it had been hard. Harder than hard.

And now… Everything came with consequences, and sometimes those consequences lasted a lifetime.

She drained her tea—lemon and ginger—and took a deep breath before heading back out towards the building.

Winter was well and truly in the air. The days were getting shorter and there was a biting feel to the air that penetrated all the layers of clothes she had put on.

Thick socks, jeans, her thermal vest, a loose, long-sleeved tee shirt, a jumper, the long scarf which could wrap three times around her neck and a woolly hat pulled right down over her ears.

She barrelled through the revolving door of the building—a bit of an anachronism considering the age of the property—and was ejected into a modern marble interior that seemed more suited to a five-star luxury hotel than an office block.

But then she imagined that Daniel never did anything by halves.

Cool shades of grey were interrupted by towering plants and a semi-circular reception desk, behind which three snappily dressed women dealt with visitors with the help of their sleek, slimline computers.

The place carried the unmistakable whiff of vast sums of money being made.

At a little after eleven in the morning there wasn't the usual early-morning throng of employees hurrying to get to their desks, but there were sufficient people coming and going to allow her a few moments of unobserved privacy, during which she thought. Thought about what lay ahead...

Should she have warned him of her arrival? Would he have scarpered rather than have a conversation with her? He was only going to be in London for a couple of months. Renovations, apparently, to the office block in which she was now standing, gazing hesitantly around her. This was her window to catch him before he disappeared to the other side of the world. She needed to talk to him, whether she liked it or not, and the element of surprise had seemed like a good idea.

But she still couldn't convert her resolve into action. Her head was telling her to get the whole thing over and done with...her feet were refusing to co-operate.

And she felt horribly underdressed for the surroundings. Everyone seemed to be in a suit and carrying a briefcase. These were people who didn't waste time dawdling. These were *Daniel's kind of people.*

Up ahead, to the left of the semi-circular reception desk, were three subtly camouflaged elevators. Towards the back she could just about glimpse what looked like a private courtyard, and she assumed the building was designed around it, so that the employees had their own little mini-park to it in during their lunch break if they didn't want to head outside and face the crowds.

Gathering her courage, she headed for the imposing reception desk.

Would he even be in?

He was.

The blonde behind the desk wasn't warm and welcoming, but she didn't ask too many intrusive questions and the one side of the conversation Delilah heard, which was obviously conducted with someone else—perhaps his secretary while he was in the country—was brief and productive.

She was given a visitor's pass, directed to the lifts—or the stairs, if she'd rather—and told to make her way to the far right wing of the building.

Apparently she wouldn't be able to miss his office because it occupied most of the right wing of the building to which she had been directed.

A Very Important Man.

She would be going to see a stranger—not the man in whose arms she had lain night after night, who had made love to her as though it was the only thing he wanted to do in the world, the only thing he'd been born to do...

And just like that she was reminded of what she had lost, for coming out of the elevator was a couple...

The dark-haired woman was small and curvy, and gazing up adoringly at the very tall, very muscular dark-haired man who was holding her close against him.

This, Delilah thought with a pang of intense longing, was the very picture of a couple deeply in love.

She brushed past them and the man glanced briefly at her, barely registering her presence. A jolt of pure shock washed through her.

Those eyes! The same arresting shade of green as Daniel's...

She turned, watching their progress out of the building. That must surely be Daniel's brother... A De Angelis who had actually opened himself up to falling in love... Because the tall, striking guy was clearly head over heels in love with the small, curvy brunette pressed to his side.

On the spur of the moment she veered away from the lift and headed towards the staircase…

Daniel pushed himself away from his desk and stood up, strolling to the window and gazing down absently at the very impressive courtyard, with its fountain and its benches and carefully tended grass, which in the depths of winter, at just after eleven in the morning, was completely empty.

He had planned on having lunch with his brother and Alexa. They had, indeed, come to see the new premises with the intention of dragging him off to one of the many wine bars scattered nearby. But that had been before his secretary had informed him that a certain Delilah Scott was in Reception, asking to see him.

He turned from the pleasant view outside and couldn't contain a certain amount of satisfaction—even if that satisfaction was tempered with disappointment.

Two months. She'd walked away from him. He got it that she'd been furious with him because he hadn't announced his identity. He'd apologised. But he might just as well have not bothered, because his apology had counted for nothing. Nor had she made any attempt to understand where he was coming from.

He was rich—very rich. Most women would have been overjoyed, after their initial annoyance, to swap a so-called drifter for a billionaire.

Not her.

And that was probably why she had lingered in his head for the length of time that she had.

Unfinished business.

It could have been avoided, and then he wouldn't be where he had been for the last couple of months…thinking about her, feeling lukewarm about getting in touch with a replacement, having cold showers on far too regular a basis...

He wondered how she was going to play it. Another little spurt of anger because he'd lied to her? Before a reluctant but inevitable move towards him?

Maybe she'd fabricate some excuse about 'just passing by' and deciding to look him up. Presumably she would have found out where his offices were via Christine and Gerry. She could have called in advance, but then that wouldn't really tie in with some random excuse about being in the vicinity, would it?

A darker thought occurred to him...

He'd offered to help her and her sister out of the financial difficulties they were experiencing. Had sufficient time elapsed that she'd had time to work out just how advantageous it would be to have him on board?

That would be disappointing, but he knew enough about women to believe that they were predictably susceptible to a bit of gold being dangled in front of them. Even the most self-righteous couldn't resist and, frankly, he hadn't met too many of those in his lifetime.

Sex for money.

No strings attached.

She was coming to take him up on the offer he'd made to her two months previously and it irked him that he was willing to let her back into his bed. He was, however, enough of a realist to accept that if he didn't she would probably continue to niggle away at the back of his mind, and that wasn't going to do.

Time was money, and he just couldn't afford the unnecessary distraction.

The office block was pretty much up and running, thanks to the amount of money he'd thrown at it. Work had begun on the cruise ship and, again, things were moving along swiftly because money talked.

He anticipated heading back to Sydney some time before Christmas, detouring via Italy so that he could spend part of the festive season with his father, his brother and Alexa.

He wondered how Delilah would accept what was now on the table—because the offer hadn't changed. A limited time in which they would indulge their mutual desire.

He gave it a couple of seconds before he responded to the knock on the door—time during which he resumed his seat behind the big mahogany desk.

Delilah, her nerves at screaming point, wanted to hide behind the secretary who was now standing by the imposing wooden door that separated her outer office from her boss's.

Smoked glass advertised Daniel's presence in his office, but all she could see was a shape.

She thought how lovely it would be if that door opened and she discovered that her memories of him were all rose-tinted and wildly exaggerated. How much braver she would feel if she discovered that he was shorter than she remembered…squatter…less *overwhelming*.

But as she was ushered into the office every single one of those hopeful conjectures was wiped out by the sight of him, sitting behind an absolutely enormous desk.

This was and wasn't the Daniel she had fallen in love with.

Same striking face…those mesmerising green eyes… and the towering, muscular body of someone genetically programmed to be lean, who worked out so that there wasn't a spare ounce of fat on him.

Same overpowering presence…

Her breathing was shallow as she absorbed all of that and then everything else that was different.

His hair was shorter, cropped close, but still the same dirty blond colour. His skin was bronzed, so that there was the same peculiar eye catching contrast between his colouring and his hair.

He was wearing a suit.

'What a surprise.' He broke the silence and nodded to the chair in front of his desk. 'Why don't you sit down? You look as though you're in danger of imminent collapse.'

Delilah licked dry lips and thankfully subsided into the chair. Now that she was here, actually in front of him, all the cool she had hoped to have at her disposal had vanished. She was a mess.

'What brings you to London?' *As if he didn't already know.* He sat forward, resting his forearms on the desk, fingers lightly linked, head tilted questioningly to one side as he looked at her in perfect silence.

'I… I needed to talk to you…'

'About what? The fate of all the crew aboard the liner? I could go into the details, if you'd like, but suffice to say they're all happy campers…' He smiled, but the smile didn't quite reach his eyes. He was remembering the strident moral high ground she had taken the last time they had been together.

'I… No, I haven't come to talk about that…but of course, yes…it seems that you've re-hired a lot of the original staff…which is really good…'

'So if you haven't come for a little catch-up, then why are you here, Delilah? The last time we spoke you were in high dudgeon, and if my memory serves me right you stormed out of my cabin shrieking that you never wanted to lay eyes on me again…'

He'd missed those floaty shapeless clothes, which were nothing like the dapper suits that surrounded him. She was as nervous as hell and he wasn't surprised. Humble pie never tasted good, and she had chewed off a very large slice.

'I wouldn't be here if I… I didn't have to be…' Delilah muttered. He wasn't going to make this easy for her. She couldn't blame him in a way. On the other hand, what would it cost him to be a just a little friendlier?

So there it was… That hadn't taken long… He should be pleased, considering he'd always been a guy to cut to the chase, as well…

'So…' he drawled, relaxing back into the chair and looking at her with brooding intensity. 'Your venture with your sister…'

'Sorry?'

'The project you and your sister have sunk all your savings into…taken out a hefty bank loan to finance…'

'What about it?'

'Oh, I'm just thinking aloud…playing around with the reason why you've shown up on my doorstep two months after you stormed out of my cabin…'

'I stormed out of your cabin for a reason! You lied to me…' She had told herself that she wasn't going to go down the road of rehashing what had happened between them and resorting to old accusations, because that wasn't going to go anywhere, but the expression on his face…

Daniel lifted one lazily imperious hand to halt her mid-accusation. 'Let's skip Memory Lane,' he advised coolly, 'and bring things back to the present. When I was told that you had shown up here and wanted to see me, I confess I was a little surprised—but it didn't take me long to figure it out…'

'Why *am* I here?' she questioned jerkily. Surely he couldn't be *that* clever at reading situations? But then the timeline should tell him something, shouldn't it?

'Money,' Daniel said succinctly.

'Sorry?'

Suddenly consumed with restless energy, Daniel vaulted upright and began striding through his office, which had been kitted out in a style that suited the age of the building. His office in Sydney was the last word in modern. This was all wood and rich tones.

Not that he noticed. He was so damned *alive* to her... huddled in the chair, watching him... He was half furious with himself for even seeing her when he knew why she had come, and half triumphant that she was here at all, in his office, on the verge of caving in.

'It took you a while...' He stopped dead in his tracks in front of her and leaned down, supporting himself by his hands on either side of her chair, caging her in so that she automatically flinched back, nostrils flaring as she breathed him in. 'But in the end you couldn't resist the lure of the big bucks...'

His forest-green eyes locked with hers and his proximity sucked the oxygen out of her lungs, leaving her gasping and panicked.

Delilah's mouth parted in bewilderment.

'You want money and I'm prepared to give it to you... We've already established what the trade-off is...' He straightened, returned to his chair behind the desk, but now he pushed it back and stretched out his long legs to one side. 'And, seeing that you've tracked me down to re-establish what we had, *I* get to choose the terms and conditions...'

Something not quite audible left her throat.

She marvelled that she hadn't foreseen this—hadn't predicted that someone as arrogant and downright egotistical as Daniel De Angelis would put a completely different spin on her unexpected arrival at his office.

He thought that she had come running back, tail between her legs, so that they could resume where they had left off! And that she'd done it because he'd dangled his wealth in front of her like a carrot!

'And what exactly are these so-called "terms and conditions"?' she asked with glacial politeness.

'You're mine for as long as I want you…' He smiled, enjoying the thought of what was to come. 'And when I say mine, I *mean* mine. You…here in London…for the next few weeks…at my beck and call… In return I guarantee that I will sort out all the financial problems you and your sister are currently experiencing…'

'What a thoughtful and generous man you are, Daniel De Angelis.' She could barely keep her voice steady. 'But it's not going to work.'

She sprang out of her chair, walked in jerky steps to the window and took a few deep breaths as she stared down at the courtyard she had glimpsed earlier when she had entered the building. It was impressive. Like everything else she had seen of the premises.

She thought back to the casual way he had arranged that supper on the deck for them, his nonchalant approach to money, the ease with which he had seemed to *own* his surroundings, the lazy charm which she had found so bone-meltingly impressive.

All the hallmarks of a man born into money, accustomed to getting what he wanted at the snap of his fingers.

'Why not?' He frowned. 'Maybe you want to fix a price? Have a piece of paper signed by me so that you know what you're letting yourself in for?'

'Do you know something?' Delilah said, her voice high and shaky. 'I'm beginning to wish that I'd never come here! I might have known that you'd think the worst of me! Do you really and truly think that I made the trip here because I wanted to ask you for *money*? Because I wanted to trade my body for *cash*?'

She pushed herself away from the window but she

couldn't be still, so instead she stalked through the office, her arms wrapped tightly around herself, her nails biting into the tender flesh of her forearms.

'I feel sorry for you,' she said through gritted teeth, pausing long enough to look at him but then looking away again, because even though she was seething with anger some detached part of her still couldn't help but appreciate his overpowering masculine beauty. 'You're so caught up thinking that every single woman must be interested in your money you won't even allow yourself to think that some might not give a damn!'

'I don't imply that they're *exclusively* interested in me because of my bank balance.' Daniel wasn't going to rise to the bait. He was too busy enjoying the hectic flush in her cheeks.

He realised that this was part of the reason why he hadn't been ready to bid her farewell ten days into their fling... She challenged him in ways other women didn't and never had. It was the sort of thing that would get tiring after a while, but he hadn't yet had his fill of it.

Delilah's colour deepened. Oh, she knew only too well what else there was about this man that attracted a woman. The way he smiled...the look and the smell and the feel of him...the way he touched...his fingers, his hands...the way his mouth traced your contours until you were going crazy with want...

She blinked back the slow motion reel of graphic images.

'I don't care about your money, Daniel, and I haven't come here to try and barter my body for cash...'

'That's an ugly way of phrasing things.'

'I'm being honest.'

She'd lingered on the word *honest* and he frowned at her.

'Are we going to go there again? I didn't board that

liner with the express purpose of finding a woman so that I could establish a relationship with her based on lies… And if you haven't come here because of the money, then why *have* you come?'

He smiled slowly at her, the sort of wolfish smile that made her toes curl.

'You've missed me…' he mused flatly. 'Have you? Missed me?'

There was just the briefest of hesitations but it was enough for him to get the message that, yes…she'd missed him.

'There's something you need to know.' She said this before she could let that hot, sexy look on his face deprive her of all conscious ability to string two words together. She wrung her hands and gazed past him, through the window to the leaden grey sky outside. 'You're probably going to hit the roof, but I couldn't *not* tell you.'

Daniel stilled.

For once his agile brain was trying and failing to join the connections that would point him in the direction of knowing what she had stored up her sleeve.

'Spit it out, Delilah,' he said, but something was telling him that, whatever she had to say, it would be something he didn't want to hear.

'I'm pregnant.'

That flat statement left behind it a deafening silence. She didn't want to look at his face because she didn't want to see the dawning horror.

Daniel's thought processes had closed down. For the first time in his life he couldn't get his head around what she had said. He wondered whether he had misheard her, but when he looked at her face, drained of colour, there was no mistaking the sincerity of what she had just told him.

Yet he still heard himself say, 'You're kidding?'

'Do you really think I've come all the way down here to see you as a *joke*?' Delilah exploded.

Sifting through the fog swirling round in his head, he caught himself drawing the conclusion that she hadn't missed him…probably hadn't given him a passing thought until she'd discovered…

'Are you sure?'

'Of course I'm sure! I did three tests, Daniel.'

'Tests aren't always right.'

'It must have happened that very first time…if you remember…'

'I remember.'

Suddenly the generous dimensions of his very large office seemed too small. *Pregnant.* She was pregnant. Having his baby. He'd not given even a passing thought to having a relationship, certainly not settling down, and now here he was: facing fatherhood.

Life as he knew it was at an end.

The silence swirled and thickened and he surfaced from his daze to see her rising to her feet.

'Where are you going?' he demanded, shooting up as well.

'I'm leaving you to think about it.'

'Have you *lost your mind*?' He looked at her in utter amazement. 'You've waltzed in here and dropped a bombshell and you're leaving so that I can *think about it*?'

'It's a shock…' Delilah mumbled, edging towards the door—but not nearly fast enough, because he was in front of her before she could reach it.

'That's the understatement of the year!'

'And before you launch into some stupid speech about me coming here to try and get money from you because I'm pregnant, I haven't. I came here to tell you because you have a right to know and that's it. I don't want *anything* from you.'

What she wanted was the one thing he was incapable of giving. Love. Affection. Joint excitement at the prospect of having a baby with her.

But having a baby with her was the equivalent of a bombshell being detonated in his life.

Nowhere in all her secret romantic fantasies had she ever envisaged her life turning out like *this*.

'I can't have this conversation here.' He flung on his coat, then moved to stand by the door, like a bouncer at a nightclub, waiting for her to follow him.

Did she want a conversation? No. But a conversation was going to be necessary—like it or not. Bombshells would do that…would instigate a question and answer session.

One thing, however… There was no way she was going to let him think that she would be turning into a freeloader just because she was carrying his baby… She wasn't going to be one of those *gold-diggers* he had to be so careful about, because he was such a rich and important human being!

'I have a train to catch,' she told him.

'And you'll catch it,' he replied, in a voice of steel, 'just as soon as we talk about this. You're not paying me a flying visit and then disappearing so that I can *think about it*…and you're certainly not jumping to any conclusions that my role in this is to have a little think and then wash my hands of the whole thing. Not going to happen. This bombshell is going to have permanent consequences— whether you like it or not…'

CHAPTER EIGHT

SHE FOUND HERSELF tripping along in his wake, out of the office building, out into the bleak grey winter and, after five minutes of walking through a confusing network of small streets, straight into the dark confines of an ancient quintessentially English pub.

Dark suited her.

'I don't make daytime drinking a habit,' he told her, settling her into a chair while he remained on his feet, 'but I feel that the occasion demands it. What would you like? And don't even *think* of doing a runner when I'm up at the bar...'

'I wouldn't...' Although the thought *did* hold a certain amount of appeal.

She watched him as he headed for the bar. He'd slung his coat over the back of a chair and she greedily and surreptitiously drank in the long, muscular lines of his body, sheathed in a handmade Italian suit of pale grey.

He was the last word in sophistication, and she couldn't help but notice how people turned and stared. He was drop-dead gorgeous, and it was a timely reminder of just how out of place she was in his world. This was the world in which *he* belonged. Not her.

'Good. You're still here.'

'I'm not going anywhere.' She took the proffered mineral water from him. 'I know we do probably need to talk, but I just want to repeat what I said to you in your office.'

She shot him a defiant look from under her lashes. God, he was so beautiful, so urbane and sophisticated and carelessly elegant, while she...

One glance at her clothes and she knew that she would be plunged into unwanted feelings of inadequacy and self-consciousness. This wasn't the cruise liner, where the standard uniform had been *dress down and casual*. This was the city, where big money was made, and there was no room for the casual look. This was *his* comfort zone.

'Not interested.'

'You need to know that I didn't come here because I want anything from you,' she repeated fiercely. 'I know you think that you're a hot catch, and that you have to be on permanent guard because there are gold-diggers out there just dying to take advantage of you—'

'No one takes advantage of me.' Daniel's mind was almost entirely consumed with a future in which he was a father. 'I'm wary because I'm a natural target.' Experience had taught him that.

'But not for me.'

'Speech over?'

Delilah gazed at him with helpless frustration. 'I thought you would have taken the news a lot more badly,' she confessed.

'You thought I'd throw a tantrum? Shout? Hit things? Not my style. This is a problem that has to be dealt with, and throwing a temper tantrum isn't going to get either of us anywhere. And before you tell me that it's *your* problem and nothing to do with me—'

'I never said that.'

'You implied it. So before you decide to venture down that road again I'll tell you straight away that this is *my* problem as well and you won't be going through it on your own.'

Tears rose readily to her eyes and she blinked them

back. She'd been feeling tearful ever since she had returned to the Cotswolds. She had put that down to the fact that she missed him, that she couldn't see a way forward with a life in which he didn't feature. Now she understood that, however much she had missed him, her hormones were all over the place.

But she still resented the way he insisted on describing the situation as a *problem,* a *bombshell.* What other awful adjectives could he dredge up? she wondered? *Disaster? Catastrophe? Nightmare?* Didn't he have *any* sensitivity at all?

'Where are you living?' he demanded bluntly.

'Back at home with Sarah.'

'And the building work?'

'There were a few delays,' Delilah muttered, feeling about as comfortable as someone being pinned to a chair and questioned with a torch shining on their face. 'Halfway through they discovered some rising damp which had to be treated, and then the whole cottage needed treating, so everything has ended up a little behind schedule...'

'Behind schedule and over-budget?' Daniel guessed shrewdly. 'And presumably in a state of upheaval?'

Delilah maintained a mutinous silence, but he raised his eyebrows until she eventually shrugged grudging agreement.

'Pregnant and trying to cope with building work and general chaos?'

'There's a time line. It'll all be done in four weeks. The builders have assured us of that...'

Daniel burst out laughing and she glared at him resentfully. 'Since when do assurances from builders count for anything?'

'*You're* having work done on the liner. Are you telling me that you don't trust the time scale?'

'I pay them so much that they wouldn't dare overrun by a second.'

'Well, bully for you.'

'I don't like the thought of you having the stress of living somewhere there are builders trooping in and out, in the depths of winter... Chances are the heating will be down at some point and it'll be beyond uncomfortable. Unacceptable.'

'Hang on just a minute—!'

'No, Delilah, *you* hang on just a minute.' He was deadly serious as his green eyes tangled with hers and he leant forward, elbows on the table, cradling his drink in one hand. 'You don't get to do what you want. You're carrying my baby and this stops being just about you.'

'I get that, but—'

'There are no *buts*.'

'I have responsibilities to my sister. We have a business to get off the ground.'

'The situation has changed.'

'You can't just lay down laws, Daniel!' She could feel the power of him steamrollering over her, knocking aside every objection she raised, inexorably pressing her into a corner from which she would have no escape route.

She could feel control of her life being taken away from her and she resented it—because this was a guy who wasn't doing it because he cared about *her*... This was a guy who was doing it in response to the bombshell that had been dropped at his door.

'What did you think would happen when you came here to see me?'

'I... I thought that I'd give you some time to think things over...'

'And how much time did you allot to that?'

'You're busy, and you'd made it clear that you and I were in it for the very short term. You enjoy your freedom. I thought you'd take a few days…maybe even a few weeks…and after that…'

'I'm all ears…'

He leaned closer towards her and the unique scent of him filled her nostrils, leaving her giddy, making her lose the string of what she'd been telling him.

'And after that we could reach some sort of arrangement—if you chose to keep in touch at all…'

Wrong thing to say. He looked at her with thunderous incredulity. *'If I chose to keep in touch?'*

'I'm not saying that you would have vanished without a backward glance…' she backtracked hurriedly. 'But there's no need for you to take an…er…an active role… Lots of men don't…'

'I don't believe I'm hearing this.'

'Daniel, you have an empire to run! I looked you up on the internet… You don't even live in this country! Of course you can take an interest, but forgive me for thinking that you might find it a little tiresome to commute from Australia every other weekend!'

'I have no intention of being a part-time father.'

Delilah looked at him in bewilderment, because she had no idea where he was going with this.

'Well, what are you suggesting?' she asked cautiously.

'Let's start with the small stuff.'

'Like what?'

'The matter of you moving out of the Cotswolds.'

'That won't happen,' she said bluntly. 'It can't.'

'Your sister must understand this change in circumstances.' He looked at her narrowly. 'Except,' he said slowly, 'she doesn't know…'

'Not yet.'

'Good heavens, Delilah!'

'Well…'

'Well? You think she's going to give you a long lecture on being irresponsible…?'

She fought against the urge to confide in him. They didn't have any kind of relationship! 'She might…'

'Does she even know about me?'

'Not exactly.'

'Is that your way of saying not *at all*?'

He was outraged and frankly insulted when she blushed and shrugged her shoulders. He could almost understand her not confiding in her sister just yet about the pregnancy. It was a huge thing, and from what she had told him about her sister a warm hug and congratulations wouldn't have been her first response. Yes, he got that she might have needed time to absorb the enormity of her situation and then steel herself for sharing that particular confidence.

But to have kept silent about *him*…

Sheer male pride, but how many women would have *hidden* the fact that they'd been seeing him? He was accustomed to women doing their best to get him along to events where they could show him off to all their friends and family!

'Why should I have told her about you?' Delilah said defensively. 'We had a little bit of fun and then we went our separate ways. It wasn't as though you were going to be a continuing part of my life!'

'Well, once the cat's out of the bag you will have to explain that you labouring on a building site in the Cotswolds isn't going to do.'

'And what about *you*?' she threw at him. 'Are you going to emigrate to London so that you can be a part of your baby's life?'

Of course not! she thought bitterly. He would dish out orders and commands, have no problem with utterly disrupting her life—as if it hadn't been disrupted enough already—but he would make sure that *his* remained relatively intact.

It would be a major decision. Daniel knew that. But was there much of a choice for him?

He knew what it was like to come from a closely bonded family, knew the importance of having a father there as a role model. It was something he would not deny his own child, whatever the cost.

'I am,' he said, coolly and smoothly, and Delilah's mouth fell open.

'How *can* you?' she asked. Caught on the back foot, she could only think that he was having her on.

'What do you mean?'

'You can't just walk away from your home in Australia…'

'Because you assume that I'm as selfish as you are?'

'That's not fair, Daniel! I have a responsibility to my sister!'

'You also have a responsibility to our child, and frankly to me as well—considering I'm the father. I can effect a hand-over process at my offices in Sydney. The world is such a global village now that it's fairly immaterial where a head office is based unless it happens to be specifically based somewhere for tax purposes. Coincidentally, I've just finished work on my London office—there's no reason why I can't operate from there and go out to the Far East as and when the occasion demands.'

He would miss his boat and the freedom of going sailing when time permitted. He would also have to start looking for somewhere to live. The family penthouse in Knightsbridge wasn't going to do.

'I am prepared to change continents. You are prepared to do *what*, Delilah? You came down here in the expectation that you would impart your information and then walk away, safe in the knowledge that I had been informed, your conscience cleared, and you could carry on as normal.'

'Hardly as *normal*!'

'You didn't expect me to want to do anything apart from maybe clock in now and again when I happened to be in the country. Am I right? Maybe set up a standing order so that you could be solvent—?'

'I don't want your money.'

Daniel overrode her interruption. If she imagined that life was going to be anything but *abnormal* now then she had another think coming, and he intended to make sure that she was given no room to squirm away from her responsibilities and the changes he knew were going to be inevitable, whether either of them liked it or not.

'Did you think that I would be a little taken aback that you were having my child but aside from that would allow you to vanish back up to the country, leaving me to get on with my life undisturbed?' He laughed mirthlessly.

'You enjoy your freedom!'

'Not to the extent that I would allow it to take precedence over my responsibilities.'

'I don't want to be your *responsibility*! Just like I don't want this pregnancy to be a *bombshell* or a *problem* that has to be fixed. Neither of us expected this, but at least *I'm* not looking at it as some sort of catastrophe that has to be put right!'

'I'm not going to get lost in an argument about semantics. We have to deal with this, and you have to take on board that it's something we'll be dealing with *together*. I'm going to move to London and so are you.'

His voice was cool and inflexible, as was his expression. She could dig her heels in and tell him to get lost but she knew he would keep her hostage in the pub until she gave in.

And, as he'd said, he was moving continents simply to

be able to see more of his child. She was uneasily aware that for her to refuse to move a few dozen miles would smack of mulish inflexibility.

She might not want him in her life because it would be hard. Seeing him would be a constant reminder of what she wanted and what she couldn't have—a constant reminder of the limitations of their relationship. But, extracting *her* from the equation, wouldn't it be a good thing for their child to have the presence of an interested and caring father?

And she would still be there for Sarah. She would be able to go up at least once or twice a week to help oversee the building project.

'I would have to find somewhere to rent in London.'

'Leave that to me,' Daniel said with silky assurance.

'And I would still want my independence,' she felt obliged to inform him, just in case he thought that he could call all the shots. That was a precedent she didn't want to encourage. He was so forceful, so overpowering, that it wouldn't take much for him to assume that what he said was irrefutable law. 'And of course I would expect you to…er…keep yours, as well…'

This was going to be a mature, civil arrangement, and it was important that he understood that, however much he was willing to adapt and contribute, she would not expect him to change each and every aspect of his life.

She wasn't going take what he offered and then cling like a limpet.

She wasn't going to let him suspect just how much she wanted from him and just how painful it was for her to accept that it was just never going to happen.

She was going to play it cool.

'What do you mean by that?'

'I mean that if you're willing to come all the way over here, so that you can have a hands-on relationship with our child, then I'm willing meet you halfway on that score and move to London—at least temporarily. I expect that as time goes on things might very well change on that front.' *Hope sprang eternal.* 'But I don't expect either of us to give up our lives entirely. You're free to carry on seeing other…er…women, and I'm free to…to—'

'Out of the question.'

'I beg your pardon?'

'The small stuff was the business of you leaving the Cotswolds. The slightly bigger stuff is the business of what I mean when I say that I want to play an active role in my child's life. That's something I can't do on an occasional basis.'

He paused so that she could digest what he was saying.

'We're not getting involved in a custody situation,' he informed her. 'You won't be out and about playing the singles game while I hang around and wait for some guy to bounce along thinking he's got paternal rights over my child. Nor will I be chasing behind women and kidding myself that I'm still a bachelor.'

Delilah could only stare at him. Bombarded by so much information, she was finding it difficult to sift through and pick out the salient points.

'And that's not going to happen,' he continued remorselessly, 'because we're going to get married.'

Delilah stared at him in utter shock. He was as cool as a cucumber, so cool that she wondered whether she hadn't imagined his outrageous suggestion.

'You've got to be kidding,' she said eventually, and he tilted his head to one side and looked at her.

'About as serious as the Bubonic Plague.'

'I'm not going to *marry* you!'

'Of course you are.'

'Oh, I am, am I? Are you going to drag me up the aisle and force me to say *I do*?'

Delilah was literally shaking with anger. Coming from a self-confessed commitment-phobe—a guy who had bluntly told her that he would only ever consider marrying into his own class, because there were so many gold-diggers out there and a guy like him couldn't be too careful—was she actually expected to take his proposal *seriously*?

'I won't have to. You're pregnant, and I can give you everything you could ever want. Both you and our child would benefit from every advantage money can buy. You would never have to work again, never have to worry about money again... You could have the sort of life you've probably only ever dreamt about...'

'It was never my dream to be rich—and I can't believe I'm hearing this!'

Daniel regarded her coolly. When she'd protested enough she would see the sense of what he was saying. She probably did now, even though she was still busy protesting.

'I have *never*,' she said in fevered whisper, 'dreamt of falling pregnant by a guy who isn't interested in a relationship! I have *never* dreamt about being someone's responsibility or putting them in a position they don't want because they've had a *bombshell* dropped in their life! And I have *never* thought that what I really want out of life is *money*.' She stood up, shaking like a leaf. 'I'm going to go now.'

'Over my dead body!' Daniel leapt to his feet.

After the token protest he had expected gratitude. Or at least some show of looking at the situation with common sense! Instead, she was acting as though he had insulted her in the worst possible way by suggesting marriage!

'You're being ridiculous!' He wanted to bellow, to shake some common sense into her. Instead, he held her by the arm as she was about to hail a taxi. 'You're not running away from me, Delilah!'

'I'll be in touch. But I won't be marrying you.'

'Why?' He raked frustrated fingers through his hair. He hadn't wanted to have this sort of conversation in his office, and he wanted to have it even less here. In the street. With the crowds swarming around them.

She looked at him with simmering resentment. 'You really don't understand, do you?'

'It makes sense.'

He looked down at her upturned face. The face that had haunted him for the past few weeks—ever since she had walked out of his life.

She still turned him on.

She was as obstinate as a mule, had rejected his offer for reasons he couldn't even begin to understand, was viewing the situation with just the sort of incomprehensible female logic he had never had any time for, and yet...

He still wanted her so badly it was like a physical ache.

And it wasn't just because this was unfinished business.

Could it be, in part, because she was carrying his child? Did he want to be a father? He'd never given it a passing thought, and yet he had to admit that there was something incredibly sexy about knowing that she carried his baby. Was it just some kind of primitive response to the evidence of his own virility?

He lowered his head and captured her mouth in an urgent kiss, his hand curving in the small of her back. He felt her melt against him. Briefly but completely. Then she pressed her palms against his chest and pushed herself away.

'Tell me that marriage doesn't make sense,' he said thickly.

Delilah was burning up, her whole body consumed by

a driving need that left her weak. How could she explain that that was *precisely* why it made no sense...*for her.*

'I'll...call you...'

'You don't have my number.'

'I have your office number.'

'That won't do. I want you to be able to reach me any time of the day or night.'

He was far from happy about her disappearing on him, and he wasn't the sort of man who had any patience at all when it came to waiting, but he could see the determination on her face and he knew that if he pushed it there was the danger that he would scare her off completely.

He gave her his number and watched as she put it into her contacts list. 'I need to be able to get in touch with you,' he said as she slipped her phone back into her bag.

Delilah looked at him with clear eyes. 'You never needed to before.'

'Things are different now.'

'I don't want to feel as though you're putting pressure on me.'

'Dammit, Delilah...!'

Their eyes met and for a few seconds her heart went out to him. He was just so endearing in his impatience, so appealing in the way he was looking at her, his green eyes alive with masculine frustration at this situation he couldn't immediately resolve.

The longing to touch him was so intense that she stuck her hands behind her back. That kiss he had dropped on her mouth was still burning, still making her realise how fast her brain cells could go into meltdown when she was with him.

'I... I'll call you,' she repeated as a black cab slowed to a stop alongside her. A black cab that would cost money she barely had.

What he was offering suddenly had such an appeal that

she had to fight against giving it house room in her head. He might be able to take care of her financially…it was true that if she married him she would never have a single financial worry in the world again…but that would be replaced by even more worries—for how on earth could she live with him when she knew that she would be waging a daily war with her own foolish feelings?

What *he* would see as a viable solution, a marriage of convenience, *she* would see as an agonising union with someone who could never return the love she felt for him.

Theirs would be a marriage of such unequal terms that it would be devastating for her mental and emotional health.

'When? I need to know…'

'In a week's time…or so…' She pulled open the taxi door before she could become embroiled in yet another debate with him. She slammed it shut and quickly rolled down the glass. 'You need time to think, Daniel, and to come to terms with the fact that I won't be marrying you…'

And then the taxi was pulling away into the impatient traffic and she was leaving him behind, already feeling the loss.

She knew that she wouldn't tell Sarah anything—not until matters had been sorted between herself and Daniel. She would confess everything as soon as they had reached some sort of solution, but at the moment a solution seemed far from being set in stone.

Move to London…

He would rent somewhere for her and she would be seeing him on a regular basis. He would be there for his child and she would be an add-on. His life would continue without her in it. Another woman would come along to absorb his attention and she wondered how she would feel when that happened.

How would she feel when, finally, he found the woman he felt he could marry? Someone rich and sophisticated?

She tried hard not to let her imagination run away with her, but over the next few days it was impossible to rein it in.

She was distracted—suddenly very conscious of all the building work happening in the kitchen, very much aware of how the disruption was beginning to get more and more unbearable. And yet she couldn't bring herself to think about leaving Sarah to get on with the project on her own.

She felt like someone wandering around in thick fog, waiting for a pinprick of light to announce a safe haven somewhere.

It was exactly a week before she contacted Daniel.

She had to brace herself for the sound of his deep, sexy drawl but when she connected with him it still took her breath away, leaving her winded.

'About time,' were his opening words.

In the middle of an important meeting he rose, signalled with a curt nod of his head that his CEO was to take over, and left the conference room without a second thought.

He'd kept many a woman waiting for the phone to ring. He'd never had the shoe on the other foot and he hadn't liked it.

It had, however, given him time to think, and he'd done a fair bit of that. He'd also put some things in motion—because at the end of the day he was a man of action. There was just so much thinking he could do, and then he needed to go beyond that point.

'Perhaps we could meet...' Delilah suggested.

'Where are you?'

'At home, of course...'

'I'll send my driver to collect you.'

'No!' She had yet to breathe a word to her sister, and the thought of some flash chauffeur-driven car pulling up outside the cottage for her sent a shiver of horror down her spine. 'I… I can come down to London…'

'When?'

'Well…'

'I'm not good at hanging around, Delilah,' Daniel told her abruptly. 'Time's passing and we need to find a way forward on this.'

'I realise that…'

'Then I suggest you get on the first train down and be prepared to stay longer than five minutes. I will ensure that my driver collects you from the station.'

'I'm perfectly capable of meeting you somewhere,' Delilah inserted quickly, because she was already in danger of handing over all control of the situation to him. He wielded power so effortlessly that it was easy to fall in with his expectation that whatever he wanted, he was entitled to get.

But, predictably, she was met at the station three hours later by his driver, and ushered to a long, sleek Jaguar with tinted windows that took her away from the bustle of the station, beyond the city and out of it.

Anxiously she dialled Daniel's number and he answered instantly.

'Where are you?' she asked.

'Waiting for you. Don't worry. You haven't been kidnapped.'

'I thought we'd be meeting…er…closer to your office…'

'Have you packed a bag?'

'I can't stay long,' she said hurriedly. 'I've told Sarah that I need to go to London for the night…'

'You're going to have to break the news to her some time.'

'I know that! Where exactly am I being taken?'

'It's a surprise.'

'I've already had my fill of surprises,' she told him honestly. 'I don't think I can stand any more.'

But, seeing that she was in his car, without the option of a quick escape, she could only sit back and watch as the clutter of the city was left behind, giving way to parks, trees, less foot traffic. It was a rare winter's day… cold, but with clear blue skies, barely a cloud in the sky.

She was delivered to a Victorian house with neat black railings outside and shallow steps leading to a black door, which was opened before she had time to bang on it with the brass knocker.

'Is this your house? Do you live here?'

His keen eyes roved over her. She was wearing so many layers that it was impossible to see whether she had gained any weight or not, but just thinking about it fired him up in a way that was sudden and powerful.

He dismissed the driver and ushered her into the house.

'Come and have a look around.'

'Why?'

'Because this is where you and our baby will be living. Here. With me.'

Delilah planted herself squarely in front of him, arms folded. 'Didn't you hear a word I said? I'm not going to marry you! And just looking at where you live shows me how different we are, Daniel! I don't come from your world and I don't want to marry into it! I *know* how you feel about women who don't come from the same background as you.' She sighed. 'What happened between us on the cruise was never meant to last. I was never the sort of woman you would have been interested in long term and just because I'm pregnant it doesn't change that. We're two people on opposite sides of a great big divide—'

'Five bedrooms, four bathrooms, countless other rooms...plenty of room for three...'

'You're *not listening*.'

'You don't want to marry me. I heard you the first time. I'm also hearing a load of rubbish about the fact that I have money and you don't.'

'It's not rubbish,' she persisted.

'Money shouldn't dictate the outcome of this situation.'

'But it will, won't it?' Delilah said bleakly. 'The man I met on that cruise was a pretend person. The real guy is here...' She looked around at the grand proportions of the house, the flagstoned flooring, the toweringly high ceilings, the priceless art on the walls. 'I don't *know* this guy...'

Daniel looked at her with a veiled expression. 'You didn't bring much with you.'

'I told you I wouldn't be hanging around.'

'No matter. I can get my guy to drive up to the Cotswolds and get whatever's necessary...'

'Necessary for what? What are you talking about?'

'We're going round in circles,' Daniel told her coolly. 'And getting nowhere fast.'

'I don't mind discussing whatever financial arrangement you want to make for the baby...'

'We need to talk about far more than that...and we can't talk here...'

'You mean in your house?'

'I want to take you somewhere special...'

'Where? Why? It doesn't matter where we have this conversation...'

'You'll need a bag...enough clothes for a couple of nights... I have a house in the Caribbean, Delilah... I want to take you there... We can relax... If you don't want to marry me I can't force you, but maybe if we're away from these surroundings we might find it easier to talk...'

He raised both hands to forestall her protest.

'It's a big villa… You can choose whichever room you want… Instead of arguing and getting nowhere we can at least try and recapture our friendship in a stress-free environment. I can't imagine how you must have felt when you discovered that you were pregnant. Money worries and then an unexpected pregnancy on top of that…tough.'

He smiled wryly and made no move to invade her space.

'A few days of sea and sand and sun might help us both find a way forward…'

Delilah's eyes widened. Little did he know it, but *he* was part and parcel of her stress. Cooped up in a villa with him? Crazy. How was *that* going to relieve her stress?

And yet wasn't he right? She felt herself getting more and more stressed by the second here. The prospect of sand and sun and sea was suddenly as powerful as the glimpse of an oasis in the middle of a desert.

Friendship. That was what they should be aiming for. The longer they argued, the less likely that was going to be. But maybe in different surroundings… Not here in London which felt frantic and claustrophobic, and not in the Cotswolds, which were all tied up with her financial worries and stress…

She found herself nodding slowly. What harm could a couple of nights do? And maybe if she could become his friend and remove the emotional attachment she would be able to deal with the situation better…

CHAPTER NINE

'Is THIS HOW you usually travel?'

In the space of one day Delilah had gone from arguing in London to sitting aboard a luxury private jet. She
felt like an intruder into a world that might have been a
different planet altogether.

With Daniel sprawled next to her she should have been
as nervous as a kitten, but somehow the minute the jet
had taken off she had felt herself relax.Daniel snapped
shut the lid of his laptop and angled his big body so that
he was facing her.

So she didn't want to talk about marriage and was adamant that he was the last person she would walk down
the aisle with?

He wasn't going to press it.

So she wanted to make a big deal of their differences?

He wasn't going to waste time arguing with her about
it. After Kelly, he'd sworn that a convenient marriage
with someone independently wealthy enough to ensure
his billions weren't the star attraction was the only kind
of marriage he would ever consider.

But life had a way of pulling the rug from under your
feet—although he'd never credited that he could ever be
the victim of *that*. Control every aspect of your life and
there could be no nasty surprises. That had been the the-
ory at any rate.

She'd given him a way out, and he knew that he could

have taken it and kept his freedom intact, but the second she had told him about the pregnancy he had known that freedom didn't stand a chance.

He wanted the whole marriage deal. He wanted his child to have both parents. He didn't want her to get involved with anyone else. He didn't want to share his child, with weekend visits and watching from the sidelines while some other guy played the daddy role.

He didn't want to share *her*.

'It doesn't tend to work when I'm in London,' he drawled, eyebrows raised. 'Troublesome getting from my house to my office in a private jet... I find the car a much better proposition.'

Delilah didn't want him to make her laugh. They were going to stay in his villa. They were going to try to become friends. She was going to have to learn to put a little distance between them. But being witty came naturally to him, and he wasn't doing it because he cared for her, or because he wanted to get anywhere with her.

'What did you tell your sister?' he asked curiously.

'I told her that I was pregnant,' Delilah said on a sigh. 'I just didn't know how much longer I could keep it to myself. I mean, if I'm going to be living in London so that you can visit the baby I had to give her some warning...'

The last thing Daniel wanted to hear was that his role was being downgraded to ex-lover with visiting rights, but arguing wasn't getting him anywhere. He gritted his teeth in a tight smile.

'And her reaction?'

'Shock. I thought she was going to faint on the spot.'

'I don't suppose her shock was as great as yours when *you* found out...'

'It was the last thing I was expecting,' Delilah agreed, staring past him through the small window. They had been served drinks as soon as the plane had taken off and she nursed the orange juice she had requested. 'I was terrified,' she admitted. 'When I thought about having a baby all I could see were problems. It was like looking down a tunnel and not seeing any light.'

She focused on him and thought… *He's a friend…an ex who, thankfully, hasn't shied away from his responsibilities…who wants to provide support…that's the main thing…*

'I never thought that I'd be a single mum. I mean, it never occurred to me at all. I thought that I might end up on the shelf—but a single mother? No…'

Daniel didn't remind her that he had asked her to marry him. He wasn't interested in hearing another litany of reasons why it would never happen.

'I didn't think you would be as supportive as you've been,' she admitted, flushing.

'Because I'm a bastard who lied to you…?'

She looked away, reminded of the idiot she'd been to have fallen in love with a man who had never been in it for the long haul.

'There's no point rehashing that,' she said with casual nonchalance. 'The main thing is that you're going to have an ongoing relationship with our child and us becoming friends is a good idea…'

She was so *aware* of him—sitting so close to her that she could just move her hand and touch his forearm, feel its muscled strength and the brush of the dark blond hair on his arms under her fingers.

Becoming friends felt like the hardest thing in the world to do, but she was going to have to do it. She wasn't going to marry him—would never marry a man who didn't love her—but she was going to have to get used to a different type of relationship with him, however hard that was going to be.

'Tell me about where we're going…' she encouraged vaguely. 'Which island is it?'

'You wouldn't have heard of it.'

'Because I'm not well travelled?' she suggested, her voice cooler. 'I did geography at school. I was actually okay at it. I do happen to know about the Caribbean, even if I don't have first-hand knowledge of any of the islands.'

'You wouldn't have heard of it because I own it.'

Delilah's mouth dropped open and she stared at him in amazed silence for a few seconds. 'You *own* an island?'

'Not exclusively,' Daniel admitted. 'It's a joint enterprise with my brother. Not that either of us has actually spent much time holidaying there.'

He was a billionaire—there was no point in trying to play it down.

She didn't say anything, and eventually Daniel broke the tense silence with a heartfelt sigh. 'You're going to tell me that it's just another example of these different worlds we inhabit.'

'It's true, though, isn't it?'

'I can't deny that I've never had much experience of financial stress. My brother and I came from a wealthy family and we've both managed to make fortunes of our own.'

'I don't know why we're bothering with this trip,' Delilah heard herself say. 'We could have sorted out the money angle back in London.'

'Back in London we couldn't sort anything out without an argument.'

'I wasn't trying to be argumentative. I was trying to be practical.'

'The truth is, I thought that you could do with the relaxation… I get it that this will have been as much of a shock to you as it is to me and stress isn't good during pregnancy. At least, I wouldn't have thought so…'

For Delilah, that made more sense. He wanted to de-stress her for the sake of the baby, and he had the sort of bottomless wealth that enabled him to do it in style. Most men would have had to make do with a meal out.

Lots of men in his position, she thought guiltily, wouldn't even have bothered with the meal out—wouldn't have thought further than grabbing the get-out clause she had offered and running away with it. But he wasn't *most men.* She wanted to hate him because he had lied to her and strung her along, but she grudgingly had to concede that there was a strong streak of honesty and decency in him. He hadn't shied away from taking responsibility and now here he was, taking her on a far-flung getaway so that she could de-stress!

She followed his reasoning. They were to become friends, and that was going to be easier away from the grit and grime of London and, yes, from the arguing.

'What does it feel like to own an island?' she asked, intrigued against her will. 'What on earth do you do with it when you're not there?'

'Rent it out,' Daniel told her. 'It commands a healthy amount of money...'

'But you don't get there often to enjoy it?'

'Work,' he said flatly. 'It's almost impossible to take the time out.'

Delilah shot him a dry look. 'What's the point of working so much that you never get to relax and enjoy the stuff you can buy with all your money?'

Daniel watched her narrowly. When he'd gone to Santorini he'd watched all those tourists and, yes, somewhere at the back of his mind had noted the comparison between himself and the laid-back holidaymakers.

When did *he* ever get to relax? He rarely took time out, and when he did he preferred solitary forms of relaxation. Sailing...skiing... Did sleeping with women count? Women were a physical release... But complete and utter relaxation? No... He hadn't ever sought them out to provide that.

'Have you ever taken a woman to the island?' she asked, hoping that it sounded like a perfectly reasonable matter-of-fact question.

'Never.'

'Why not?'

'I marvel that I'd managed to forget how many "No Trespassing" signs you like to barge past...' But his voice was wry rather than belligerent.

'Friends know things about one another.'

'Especially friends who have enjoyed fringe benefits...?'

Delilah went bright red, and just like that her body fell into its familiar pattern, with her nipples pinching and tightening, her palms growing clammy with perspiration, and between her legs that hot ache that seemed to control all her senses until it was the only thing she was aware of.

'That feels like a long time ago.' She casually dismissed his husky suggestive remark and offered him a bright smile. 'Things are different between us now.' She cleared her throat and slanted her eyes away from his. 'So, when you've been to this island you've gone on your own?'

'Why not? It's great for snorkelling. It's surrounded by a reef and the water is very clear and very calm, The fish are so lazy and tame that they'd share your lunch with you if you gave them half a chance.'

'And you prefer to do all that on your own...?'

'I don't need a woman to spoil the peace by demanding attention and shrieking every time a fish gets too close...' he drawled.

'So what if *I* shriek when a fish gets too close?'

'You're different,' he commented drily. 'You're not

just any woman. You're the mother of my child… You should try and get some sleep now. We don't land on the island… We land on a runway on the mainland and take a helicopter from there. It's a long trip, all told…'

In other words he was no longer interested in chatting and he wasn't interested in her nosy questions.

Delilah shrugged and turned away. She knew that he had reopened his computer and could hear the steady sound of his fingers brushing against the keyboard, composing emails, reviewing important documents, doing all those things that kept him so busy that he seldom took time out to relax.

It was another mark in his favour that he was taking the time out now, when he didn't have to.

He was doing it because she was different… She was no longer a woman…she was the mother of his child. Her status had been elevated, but she missed being a woman he couldn't keep his hands off…

In the end she slept through most of the flight. When she opened her eyes the sky was bright blue outside the window and she straightened and peered past him to the banks of white wispy clouds.

'Are you excited?' she asked breathlessly, and he smiled at her.

'I think you'll enjoy the place.'

'Do you get excited about *anything*, Daniel?' she heard herself persist.

'I have my moments…' he murmured, green eyes locked on hers. 'Your hair's all over the place…'

He itched to brush it back from her face. He'd watched her as she slept and the urge to touch her had been overwhelming. He had amazing detailed recall of every inch of her body. Even before she had turned up at his office and announced the life-changing news that she was carrying his child she had managed to get under his skin in a way no other woman ever had.

She had preyed on his mind after she'd left. Why? Because, he'd told himself, she was unfinished business and he was egotistical enough to want to finish with a woman rather than the other way around. Egotism wasn't a good trait, but it was something he could deal with.

So he hadn't been able to get her out of his head…

So he hadn't been interested in replacing her with any of the women in his proverbial black book, who would have been overjoyed to have taken up where Delilah had left off…

It was just because they'd met under unusual circumstances. It was just because she'd had no idea of his true identity and he'd relished the freedom that had given him.

After his experiences with Kelly he had erected so many defences systems around himself and around his emotions that he hadn't recognised when his defences had been breached and she had breached them.

And he didn't mind.

In fact he liked it—liked it that she wasn't intimidated by him or impressed by his money.

When she had shown up in his office he hadn't been tempted to get rid of her. He'd formulated all sorts of reasons for her being there and rehearsed all sorts of arguments as to why he would be willing to take her back to his bed…where it felt as if she belonged…

The bottom line was that he'd never stopped wanting her. And more than that…

He'd watched her sleep, head drooping on his shoulder. He'd felt the soft brush of her hair against his mouth. Hell…

How was he supposed to have recognised the signs of something that was more than lust? He'd been in total control of his emotions for so long—how could he have been tuned in to the signs of anything that ran deeper than that?

And wasn't that why he was so adamant that there was no way he was going to let her go? No way that she would be able to walk away from him into the arms of someone else?

Just the thought of another man laying a hand on her filled him with sickening, impotent rage, and he'd had a lot of thoughts along those lines when she had disappeared back up to the Cotswolds. Pride had stopped him from pursuing her. That would have been a step too far. But she was here now and she was going to stay.

For the first time in his life, though, he had no idea what the rules of this game were. She didn't want him. He couldn't get to her through his money because she wasn't greedy and she wasn't materialistic, and he had lied to her. She was willing to try and forge a truce with him, but he knew that if he wanted more then he would have to use every trick in the book to get it.

And he did want more.

He just wasn't sure what those tricks to get it might entail.

Proceeding slowly—something that was anathema to him—seemed to be the only approach.

Delilah shoved her hair into something less chaotic and edged as far away from him as was physically possible.

The plane was coming in to land and she craned her neck to drink in everything as it descended and then bumped along a runway that was bordered by small hangars and beyond that waving palm trees.

As soon as the engine purred to a complete stop the heat seemed to invade the small cabin space and she was glad that she'd worn something light…a pair of cotton trousers and a loose-fitting sleeveless top.

'I feel almost guilty being here,' she confided as they headed out of the plane to make a smooth connection with a waiting helicopter. People bustled around them… the captain stopped to chat with Daniel…their bags were trundled in searing heat to the helicopter.

'Don't,' he commanded, looking down at her. 'You're pregnant and I don't want you to be stressed over anything. Or to feel guilty because you're here. Did your sister try and imply that it was somehow *wrong* for you to take a few days away?'

He helped her into the helicopter and then heaved his big body in alongside her, the two of them cramped in the confined space. The door was slammed down, locking them into the sort of intimacy that fired up all her senses.

She licked her lips and shook her head. 'Of course not. She understands the turmoil I'm going through…'

'And she agreed that the ex-lover you refuse to marry should be the one to try and help you with that?'

Delilah was spared having to answer that by the loud whirring of the helicopter blades as the aircraft tilted up and buzzed like a wasp, hovering and then swooping along, offering a breathtaking sight of navy blue sea and turquoise sky.

'Well?' Daniel prompted as the helicopter whirred to a shuddering stop on the island.

The flight had taken a matter of minutes and here they were. It was lush and green and a four-wheel-drive SUV was waiting for them on the airstrip. As far as the eye could see there was untouched beauty and the smell of the sea was pungent and tangy. She breathed in deeply and slowly and half closed her eyes, enjoying the heat, the slight breeze and the unique tropical sounds of unseen insects and birds.

'I can't believe this is all yours.' She opened her eyes, turned full circle and gazed at him.

'It's a small island,' Daniel said drily, ushering her towards the car while, behind them, she heard the helicopter begin to whirr into life, ready to lift off and go back to the mainland.

'But still…it's just so amazing…'

Privately, Daniel had never been able to stay longer than a handful of days on the island. Boredom would inevitably set in, even though the water sports were second to none.

'What else is there? Just a villa? I can't believe you don't come here as often as you can…'

She looked at him and then through the car window and then back at him, not knowing where to feast her eyes. Swaying coconut trees lined the sides of the road and through the tall, erect trunks she could make out slivers of blue, blue sea.

When everything had been worked out between them and some sort of visiting timetable arranged, she wondered how she would ever be able to compete with this. She had a vivid image of their child coming to a place like this for a holiday and then returning to England to spend the rest of the time with her in whatever modest house she might be living in.

And then she imagined their child coming here with Daniel and whatever partner had entered his life—maybe even one of those 'suitable' women. Because, with a child, he would doubtless be anxious to settle down and find himself a wife.

Had she done the right thing? She had stood her ground and refused to let him sacrifice his life because a mistake had happened, because she had fallen pregnant. She had refused to compromise when it came to love and the right reasons for entering into a marriage with anyone.

But now doubts began to gnaw away inside her. Worriedly she shoved them aside.

Ahead of them, the bumpy road was taking them up a small incline, and as the Jeep rounded the corner her mouth dropped open at the sight of the sprawling villa ahead of them. Banked by coconut trees and every shade of green foliage she could possibly have imagined, it was a one-storeyed building that was circled by a wide, shady veranda. Impeccably maintained lawns surrounded it on all sides, and as the car ground to a halt a plump dark-skinned woman emerged at the front door and several other members of staff spilled out from behind her.

Delilah thought that this must be what it felt like to be a member of royalty. Daniel took it all in his stride. He chatted with the woman, Mabel—who, he explained, looked after the house and all the staff when it was occupied, and made sure it was kept up to scratch when it was empty, coming three times a week from the mainland to check everything over.

'Your bedroom...' he paused and nodded to one wing of the massive villa '...is there. Mine is in the opposite wing. I'll get Mabel to show you to your room and then we can have some dinner and hit the sack. It's been a long day.'

So this was what it felt like to be friends. This polite, smiling man, who had once touched every part of her body, was now offering her the hand of friendship—which she had insisted on—and she hated it.

'Tomorrow,' he said, 'I'll give you a tour of the island, but don't expect anything much longer than half an hour. There are plenty of coves and small beaches. We can have a picnic on one of them...'

'And talk about how we handle this situation?' Delilah said with a wooden smile. 'Good idea. And it was a good idea to come here,' she conceded truthfully. 'I haven't felt so relaxed since I found out that I was pregnant.'

Daniel inclined his head to one side and shoved his

hands in his pockets. Even with her clothes sticking to her, and clearly tired after the convoluted journey that had brought them here, she still had that impossible certain *something* that fired him up.

And she showed zero sign of wanting anything more than a civilised conversation about technicalities. The girl who had given herself to him with abandon was gone.

'You never told me what your sister said when you informed her that you would be coming here with me...'

'I didn't tell her that we would be going abroad.' Delilah flushed and looked away. 'I just told her that I needed to spend a few days in London because I needed to sort some stuff out with you, and that we would probably have to visit a lawyer at some point to make our agreement legal...'

'I see...'

He didn't. And what he heard was the sound of her walking away from him. The way she hadn't been able to meet his eyes when she'd said that spoke volumes. He had asked her to marry him and, whatever excuses she had come up with, the bottom line was that she didn't want him in her life, and she felt guilty about her rejection because she was fundamentally such a warm, caring, genuine person.

And there was nothing he could do about it except play this waiting game and hope.

Delilah drew her knees up and gazed out at the distant horizon, which was a dark blue streak breaking up the cloudless milky blue of the sky and the deeper, fathomless blue of the ocean. The sand underneath her was powdery white and as fine as icing sugar.

Ground up coral from the reef that surrounded the island and the reef itself were responsible for the wealth of tropical fish, which were as tame as Daniel had predicted—bright flashes of yellow and turquoise and pink that weren't afraid to weave around her in the water.

It was paradise.

She should have been over the moon.

She was surrounded by the most amazing natural beauty. Water so clear that you could wade out for absolutely ages and still see your feet clearly touching the sand. Staff on hand to serve their every whim. The food was exquisite...

And Daniel had been nothing but conscientious. No longer the flirty, charming guy who had teased her and made her laugh, but guarded and serious.

They had talked about financial arrangements and agreed that getting lawyers involved would be a waste of time, because it was important to maintain the friendship they were so successfully cultivating.

The friendship that had replaced the fun and the sex.

'You're going to get burnt.'

Delilah spun round to see him striding towards her, a towel casually draped over his broad, tanned shoulders, his bathing trunks low-slung and emphasising the glorious muscularity of his body.

They'd been on the island for two days, and it wasn't getting any easier trying to hide the effect he still had on her.

'I'll be fine.' She smiled tightly at him and quickly averted her eyes. 'We're only going to be here for another couple of days, and I'm not going to waste this sun by sitting in the shade all the time. Besides, I've lathered myself with sunblock.'

Daniel steeled himself against the cool dismissal in her voice and draped the towel on the sand and lay down next to her.

Two days and he'd got nowhere at all. He'd never felt so impotent in his life before, and he didn't know what to do about it. She smiled, listened to what he said, seemed to take an interest in all the boring historical facts he dished out about the island, asked questions about the staff and the running of the place, but the polite mask never slipped.

Because it wasn't a mask.

He should never have lied to her. It had seemed perfectly reasonable at the time—a harmless piece of fiction that he could turn to his advantage. Except things had got out of hand, and by the time she'd discovered the truth they had both overstepped more boundaries than he liked to imagine.

She had made inroads into him without his even realising it, and when she had walked away pride had stopped him from going after her.

She had had time to come to conclusions about him that he was helpless to set straight.

Frustration tore through him.

'This heat is fiercer than you think,' he gritted. 'And the last thing either of us needs is for you to come down with sunstroke.'

Delilah's temper flared and she welcomed it. After two days of stilted politeness she had a churning sea of emotion inside, desperate for an outlet.

'I don't think I need you telling me what I should and shouldn't do,' she snapped. 'I appreciate that you've taken time away from work to come here on a rescue mission to get me to relax, but don't worry... I won't set back your timetable for squeezing me in by inconveniently coming down with sunstroke...'

'There's no need for the drama, Delilah,' he drawled, his mouth tightly compressed.

'I'm not being dramatic,' she returned in a high voice. She could barely look at him, and was angrily aware of just how easy it would be to lose herself in his extravagant good looks.

Hadn't he demonstrated, without having to say a word, just how detached he had become from her?

She was overwhelmed by the hateful feeling that she was being patronised.

Or maybe it was more than that.

Her thoughts veered off at a dangerous tangent and a series of heated assumptions were made. She'd thought that he'd been wildly generous in asking her here on this little break, was being understanding about the stress she had been through. And even though she had constantly reminded herself that this wasn't about *her*, the gesture had fed into her weakness for him. That was why it had been unbearable dealing with his politeness—that was why every solicitous helping hand had been a dagger through her heart.

Because she hadn't seen him for what he was and truly accepted it.

He had dropped all talk of marriage and had distanced himself. Maybe he thought that if he was too much like the Daniel she had hopped into bed with she might be encouraged into getting ideas into her head. He had proposed out of duty and responsibility, but she was sure that he must be quietly relieved to have been let off the hook.

And then there was the fact that he had brought her *here*. Not just on a little weekend break somewhere, but *here*. To an island he *owned*, where everything from the cool, elegant bedroom, with its bamboo furniture, to the exquisite infinity pool overlooking the sea, was the very last word in what money could buy.

Had he wanted to remind her how far apart their worlds were?

He intended to take an active interest in his child's life, but was this his subtle way of showing her that with marriage no longer on the agenda they were, as she had painfully pointed out to him, poles apart?

Suddenly it seemed very important that they talk about all the things they had somehow not got around to discussing.

Rigid with tension, she looked at him, relaxing on the towel like a man without a care in the world. She stuck on her oversized sunglasses and took a couple of stolen seconds to just look at him, lying there with his eyes closed against the glare of the sun.

'We haven't really decided anything...' She broke the silence tersely. 'And I'd quite like to get things sorted so that I can enjoy the rest of my time here without all that hanging over my head.'

Daniel opened his eyes and looked at her. 'Where do you want to start?'

'I've agreed to move down to London to accommodate you, so I guess I should know what the living arrangements will be...' Delilah wondered whether that concession had been the worst decision of her life.

'You'll have an apartment or a house—whatever you want and wherever you want it to be.' Daniel loathed this conversation, which smacked of finality. 'And naturally you will have a generous allowance...'

'I'm not asking for money from you,' Delilah said in a stilted voice. 'You can just pay maintenance for our child, like any other normal person.'

'But I'm not *a normal person*, am I? I'm extremely wealthy. and neither my child nor the mother of my child will ever want for anything.'

'And if...it's early days yet...if for some reason this pregnancy doesn't work out...'

I'll still want you in my life... That was what Daniel thought, with shocking immediacy.

'Then you can have your apartment back and I'll return to the Cotswolds...'

Her heart constricted and she was ashamed to realise that she would rather see him and suffer than never see him in her life again. How pathetic was *that*?

She twisted the knife inside her. 'Although maybe I'll stay in London and find somewhere else to live. Sarah will have become accustomed to my not being around, and in London I can...'

'Find a better job? A better life? Better dating scene? Mr Right?'

Daniel smiled coldly and Delilah flinched, because he just didn't give a damn, did he?

'Maybe all of those things,' she returned defiantly. 'Why not? But I'm not going to think about that. We'll have a baby together and sort out the details and then we'll both be free to go our separate ways. Will you want whatever's agreed to be legally put into writing?'

'Will you?' Daniel enquired, restless with a savage energy that was pouring through him like toxic waste. 'Do you think I'm the kind of man to give you something with one hand while keeping the other hand free to snatch it all back at a later date?'

He vaulted upright in one swift, graceful movement and stared down at her.

With the glare of the sun behind him, his face was thrown into a mosaic of shadows and angles and she was grateful for the oversized sunglasses hiding her eyes.

'I'll email my lawyer today,' he said, with considerable cold restraint. 'And have something drawn up for signing as soon as we return to London.'

'And visiting rights?'

'As many as I like,' Daniel gritted. 'And I'm warning you, Delilah, if you fight me on this I'll fight you back. In the courts if necessary.' He smiled coolly. 'And now that we understand one another, and the details have been worked out, I'm going for a swim—you can enjoy what remains of our time here without anything "hanging over your head…"'

CHAPTER TEN

DELILAH WATCHED HIM worriedly as he swam out, further and further. until he rounded the cove and disappeared from sight.

Of course he knew this island like the back of his hand! Didn't he? He might only have come to the place a handful of times…fewer than that, probably…but he wasn't a complete idiot. Just the opposite. He would know all about currents and the dangers of getting out of his depth.

She waited for fifteen minutes, her eyes glued to the distant horizon, reluctant to go back into the house until she could see him swimming back towards shore.

The sun was fierce and after a while she sidled under a coconut tree, where she tried hard to relax although her eyes kept flickering to the shore.

Eventually, after half an hour, she gave up and trudged back up to the house—where the first person she bumped into was Mabel, who was busying herself with cleaning.

'Mabel…' She hovered, feeling foolish in her swim-suit and sarong. The staff who looked after the huge villa and took care of the sprawling grounds, were friendly and smiling but kept a respectful distance.

Mabel turned to her, her broad smile going some way to putting Delilah at her ease.

'You should get out of those wet clothes, miss. You

change and give them to me and they'll be back in your room by this afternoon.'

'Er... I just wondered... What's the sea like on the other side of the island?'

Mabel's smile wavered, and Delilah couldn't blame the poor woman for her confusion.

'Because...' She hunted for a reason that wouldn't sound completely crazy. 'Because it looks so...so tempting to just swim round the corner and see what the other beaches are like...'

'I wouldn't, miss...'

'Why not?'

'The sea out here is unpredictable, miss, and once you get past the reef... Well...'

'Well, what?' Delilah smiled encouragingly.

'Sharks, miss... Barracuda... All sorts of things... And the water ain't calm, like it is close to the shore. So it's best for you to stay in the cove—or else Mr Daniel can drive you to some of the other coves... I could make a nice picnic lunch...'

Delilah smiled weakly. She had never been a strong swimmer, and she knew that she was seeing all sorts of potential dangers in a situation that *she* would have found threatening. Daniel was a man of considerably more experience than her. He was muscular, athletic...a man built to overcome hazardous conditions.

Hadn't he told her about all those black runs he had skied down? The surging, stormy seas he had successfully navigated in his boat where he lived in Australia?

But when, after two hours, he still hadn't made an appearance, worry began to set in with a vengeance.

She couldn't relax by the pool. She'd spread her towel on a chair, but the gorgeous view of the ocean, the blue sky, the softly swaying coconut trees that bordered the land on both sides, could not distract her from the niggling suspicion that she had engineered an argument that had irritated him to the point where he had disappeared into the ocean. And God only knew where he was now.

Probably safe and sound and heading back to the house. When she looked at it logically, she thought he'd probably made it to the next beach and was calmly relaxing and thinking things through.

It wasn't as if they hadn't *needed* to talk about what they had talked about. Sooner or later they would have *had* to sit down and discuss future arrangements. And, frankly, hadn't she seen just the sort of person that he was? He had *threatened* her, for heaven's sake! Had told her that if she did anything to try and curtail his visiting rights he would fight her—and it hadn't been an empty threat.

He was willing to play the good guy, but there was no way he would allow her to cross him, so if he had stormed off in a rage because she hadn't carried on being amenable and pliable then *tough*.

They were both dealing with a difficult situation, and if she hadn't been firm and businesslike then she would have sleepwalked into him taking charge of everything. Just as he had tried to take charge when he had asked her to marry him!

Had she agreed to marry him—had she *given in* to that treacherous little voice in her head that had urged her to take what was on offer even if it wasn't ideal. because it was better than nothing and because it would allow her the forbidden luxury of still being a part of his life—she would have ended up as nothing more than an appendage, to be tactfully sidelined when the urge to sleep with other women became more pressing than the novelty of being a daddy.

That was precisely what would have happened—although she conceded he would have been diplomatic about it, would have made sure that any outside life was kept far from the prying eyes of the press. But he wouldn't have cared if *she* had known, because that would have been the unwritten codicil when they took their wedding vows. Marriage not for love but through necessity, and therefore not a marriage at all—at least not in the way she understood marriage to be!

And if she hadn't liked it—well, doubtless he would have shown her that tough, uncompromising side of him that she had already glimpsed.

She had a light lunch by herself in the kitchen. Mabel fussed around her but asked no questions about Daniel and why he wasn't there.

Delilah had no idea what she or any of the other members of staff thought about their peculiar sleeping arrangements. The fact they had come together but slept on opposite sides of the house. Did they gossip about that? Or maybe the super-rich who rented the property had their own peculiar arrangements so everyone who worked there was more than accustomed to odd sleeping situations. Who knew?

At night, the staff were all either collected and taken by boat back to the mainland or else they stayed in the collection of well-appointed little houses that formed a clutch at one end of the island. By the time six-thirty rolled around most of them had already disappeared.

There would be a delicious meal for herself and Daniel waiting in the kitchen, she knew. He didn't like anyone hovering around in the evening, waiting to collect their plates, and so, after the first night, he had allowed all the domestic staff to leave early—including the two girls who worked in the kitchen.

With no sign of him, and with darkness encroaching in the abrupt way that it did in the tropics, Delilah could bear the tension no longer.

It was a small island, and she was sure that she would be able to make her way to the next beach without getting lost. In fact it was practically impossible to get lost. But it made sense to wait until the place was empty, because although the staff might not be curious she knew that they might set out on a search party if she went missing.

The temperature had cooled by the time she quietly let herself out, pausing only to get her bearings and then purposefully walking in the direction she hoped would take her to the adjoining cove. She had a powerful torch, although the moon was full and it was bright enough for her to see without switching the torch on at all.

She had no idea how long she walked. At some point it occurred to her that she should probably return to the house soon—fortunately she had made sure to keep the lights on, so that she could orientate herself without too much difficulty. It didn't matter if they'd become fainter. As long as she could make them out in the distance she knew that she could return safely.

Getting lost wasn't a problem. Becoming exhausted, however, was, and it was so lovely and balmy, with just the softest stirring of a breeze and the soothing sounds of little insects, like peaceful, harmonious background music, that she decided to rest.

She'd changed into a pair of jeans and a tee shirt, and she was perfectly comfortable when she found herself a little mound of grass, where she nestled down and rested her legs.

She dozed.

It was impossible not to, because an overload of stress

had tired her out even more than walking the miles she had covered without realising it.

A loud crashing through the undergrowth woke her up with the unwelcome ferocity of a bucket of ice-cold water, and for a few seconds she was completely disorientated. She could still see through the trees and the bushes, and she could still hear the harmless sounds of the insects and the distant repetitive rolling of the sea, but she had no idea where she was until it all came back to her in a rush.

Daniel was missing.

She didn't care what they had said to one another. She just wanted him to be *safe* and she didn't think he was.

She struggled to her feet, backing away from the approaching noise, the sound of something methodically making its way towards her, and only heard his voice when she had spun around vainly, searching for the lights that would advertise the location of the villa.

'What in God's name are you doing here?' Daniel thundered, bringing her to a stop and probably, she thought frantically, disturbing every single member of staff who had chosen to stay on the opposite side of the island.

He stood in front of her like an avenging angel, hands aggressively on his hips and his body leaning forward, taut with belligerent accusation.

'I...' Relief washed over her and she just wanted to race forward and throw herself into his arms.

'Midnight stroll on an island you know nothing about?' he roared.

'There's nothing dangerous here! You said so yourself! No snakes...no big lions or tigers! You laughed when I told you that I'd be terrified of scrambling through all this bush on my own!'

'So you decided to put it to the test and find out whether

it was true or not?' He took a few steps closer to her. 'I've
been worried sick about you!'

'Then you shouldn't have just jumped in the sea and
swum away like that!' Her heart was racing, every sense
heightened to breaking point.

'Dammit, Delilah, why do you think I did that?'

'Because you didn't want to talk about…about the
arrangements for after I have the baby…' *Not unless
those arrangements suited him—not unless he could
have exactly what he wanted without her putting up any
arguments…*

'And why do you think *that* was?' Daniel asked
roughly.

He raked his fingers through his hair and glared at
her. Coming back to the villa…realising that she wasn't
there…he'd never felt so panicked in his life before. He'd
been sick with fear.

What if something had happened to her? It would have
been *his* fault. His fault for laying it on too thick because
he'd been in a situation he hadn't been able to handle. Had
he forced her into running away? He'd wondered whether
she had gone to the staff houses—gone to see whether
she could get one of them to take her back to the mainland on one of the boats that were kept anchored there,
to be used if the need arose.

'Forget about dangerous animals! You could have
fallen! Hurt yourself! You don't know the layout of this
place!'

'And how do you think *I* felt?' Delilah yelled accusingly. 'You just took off! You didn't come back. I… I was
worried. You went swimming. Anything could have happened. I thought I'd come out here and look for you…see
if you'd swum to another cove…'

She didn't reveal the other more terrifying scenarios

concocted in her imagination. That he was lying in one of the coves, washed up and half dead.

'I was frightened,' she confessed with a hint of defiance.

Daniel looked at her, holding his breath.

'Were you?' He exhaled deeply. 'Because *I* was,' he muttered.

He took her hand and led her out of the clearing in which she had fallen asleep. It took them under ten minutes to get to one of the many coves scattered on the perimeter of the island, and during that brief walk there was nothing Delilah could find to say.

He had been worried.

Not about *her,* she made a point of telling herself. About the baby she was carrying...

But he was holding her hand...

Was it because he was scared she might trip and fall and somehow hurt the baby? Was that it?

She was dismayed at how pleasurable it was to dwell on an alternative explanation...

'I had no idea how close I was to the sea,' Delilah said. 'I mean, I could hear it but...'

'In the dark it's confusing just how far or how close you are because the island's so small...'

She shook her hand free and walked to the water's edge, kicking off her flip-flops so that the sea, as warm as bath water, could lap over her feet. She stared out at the ocean, silvery black and ominous, but every corner of her mind was tuned in to his presence behind her, and she drew her breath in sharply as she felt him approach her from behind, so that he was standing a few inches behind her.

'I shouldn't have disappeared,' he said softly.

'Where did you go for all that time?' She didn't turn

around. It was easier to talk like this, when she wasn't drowning in his eyes and having her brains scrambled.

'There's a very small inlet on the east side of the island. I remembered it from way back. I swam there. I needed to…think…'

'I'm not going to stop you from seeing our child. You didn't have to threaten me like that.'

'I know and I… I'm sorry. Will you look at me? I want to see your face when I…when I say what I feel I must say…'

Delilah slowly turned around and looked up at him reluctantly, because she really didn't want to hear what he had to say now that he had cooled down. She didn't want any more talk about signing things and lawyers.

'I'd never drag you through the courts,' he said gruffly. 'I said that in the heat of the moment because I was just so…so damned frustrated.' He shook his head but was driven to stare back at her, at her beautiful upturned face. 'I brought you here because…'

Delilah waited, confused, because he was a guy who was never lost for words. 'Because you wanted me to relax,' she reminded him.

'Because I wanted to take time out and show you that I could be the man you wanted…in your life permanently.'

'We've been through this…' But her heart still leapt, because she'd thought he'd stopped wanting to marry her. Yes, she'd told herself that she wasn't going to marry anyone for the wrong reasons… But it still kick started a thrilling response deep inside her, like a depth charge going off.

'We're good together, Delilah…and it's not just about the sex. Even though…' he couldn't stop his voice from lowering to a sexy, husky whisper that sent shivers racing up and down her spine…the sex is the hottest sex I've ever had…'

'You don't mean that,' she was constrained to point out. 'You haven't been near me since... Not that it matters... But all that lust stuff...'

'Have you wanted me to?' Daniel interjected. 'To touch you? Because I've wanted to—so very badly—but I didn't want to scare you away. You felt that you'd ended up with a man who'd lied to you and I couldn't take that back. But I wanted to... No, I *needed* to show you that I'm no bastard. I learnt a tough lesson years ago and it hardened me. I never thought that you or any other woman would ever come along and make me question all the things I'd taken for granted...'

'Things like what?' Delilah whispered.

'Things like how emotions could get the better of me... like how I could fall in love with someone and want her so badly that the thought of not having her near me every day for the rest of my life would be beyond endurance...'

'You *love* me?' She could barely whisper that in case she'd misheard.

'I love you and I want to marry you... And I want you to believe me when I tell you that I'll never lie to you again, that I'm good for you...'

She flung her arms around him. She wanted to hold him so tightly that he would never be able to leave. She wanted to superglue him to her.

'I love you so much, Daniel. You're everything that doesn't make sense, but I fell in love with you—and that's why I knew that I couldn't marry you. Because I hated the thought of you being trapped into being shackled to me when you weren't capable of attaching emotionally.' She pressed her head against his chest and felt the steady beating of his heart. 'You can't imagine how tempted I still was to accept your proposal...except then you stopped asking and I was gutted...'

She felt him smile into her hair. 'Like I said, I didn't want you diving for cover because I had no idea how far you'd dive, and I couldn't risk you going anywhere I couldn't follow. My darling, I love you so much… Will you do me the honour…?'

Delilah grinned. She didn't think she would ever stop grinning.

'Just try and stop me,' she murmured, brimming over with happiness.

* * * * *

If you enjoyed reading Daniel's story,
you'll love his brother Theo's:
WEARING THE DE ANGELIS RING
Available now!

COMING NEXT MONTH FROM
HARLEQUIN *Presents*.

Available February 16, 2016

#3409 THE ITALIAN'S RUTHLESS SEDUCTION
Rich, Ruthless and Renowned
by Miranda Lee

Sergio Morelli has always taken what he wants—except his stunning stepsister Bella Cameron, no matter how much he desired her! Now, as Bella seeks refuge at their family home, Sergio decides it's finally time to quench the fire...

#3410 A FORBIDDEN TEMPTATION
by Anne Mather

Jack Connolly isn't looking for a woman—until he meets Grace Spencer! Trapped in a fake relationship to safeguard her family, Grace knows giving in to Jack would risk *everything* she holds dear... But will she surrender to the forbidden?

#3411 AWAKENED BY HER DESERT CAPTOR
by Abby Green

Sheikh Arkim wants revenge after cabaret dancer Sylvie Devereux costs him his respectable reputation. Luring her to his desert palace, he plans to get seductive Sylvie out of his system. But there's one secret Arkim's not prepared for...her innocence!

#3412 CARRYING THE KING'S PRIDE
Kingdoms & Crowns
by Jennifer Hayward

Prince Nikandros is about to be crowned when the royal rebel discovers the consequences of his last night with beautiful Sofía Ramirez. Whisking pregnant Sofía to Akathinia at once, the prince *will* legitimize his new rule...with a wife and child!

HPCNM0216RA

#3413 A VOW TO SECURE HIS LEGACY
One Night With Consequences
by Annie West

When usually cautious Imogen believes she's living on borrowed time, she blows her savings on a trip around the world, meeting sexy Parisian Thierry Girard. But when there are permanent consequences to their affair, Thierry imprisons her...with a gold ring!

#3414 BOUND TO THE TUSCAN BILLIONAIRE
One Night With Consequences
by Susan Stephens

Gardener Cassandra Rich captures tycoon Marco di Fivizzano's attention the moment he sees her! In her boss's arms Cass blossoms as she finds the freedom she craves—but when she discovers she's pregnant, she realizes she's bound to the billionaire forever!

#3415 REQUIRED TO WEAR THE TYCOON'S RING
by Maggie Cox

Seth Broden needs one deal to fulfill his ambitions—but to close it he must have a wife! After meeting penniless Imogen, Seth proposes a mutually beneficial arrangement... Imogen was saving herself for her wedding night, but will she be the tycoon's wife in more than name only?

#3416 THE SECRET THAT SHOCKED DE SANTIS
The Throne of San Felipe
by Natalie Anderson

Army lieutenant Stella Zambrano's life changes forever when she realizes she's pregnant. Her baby bombshell is the result of a sensual afternoon with Prince Eduardo De Santis... And with an out-of-wedlock heir on the cards, the playboy prince will demand marriage!

YOU CAN FIND MORE INFORMATION ON UPCOMING HARLEQUIN® TITLES, FREE EXCERPTS AND MORE AT WWW.HARLEQUIN.COM.

HPCNM0216RB

REQUEST YOUR FREE BOOKS!

HARLEQUIN

Presents®

2 FREE NOVELS PLUS
2 FREE GIFTS!

PASSION GUARANTEED SEDUCTION

YES! Please send me 2 FREE Harlequin Presents® novels and my 2 FREE gifts (gifts are worth about $10). After receiving them, if I don't wish to receive any more books, I can return the shipping statement marked "cancel." If I don't cancel, I will receive 6 brand-new novels every month and be billed just $4.30 per book in the U.S. or $5.24 per book in Canada. That's a saving of at least 13% off the cover price! It's quite a bargain! Shipping and handling is just 50¢ per book in the U.S. and 75¢ per book in Canada.* I understand that accepting the 2 free books and gifts places me under no obligation to buy anything. I can always return a shipment and cancel at any time. Even if I never buy another book, the two free books and gifts are mine to keep forever.

106/306 HDN GHRP

Name	(PLEASE PRINT)	

Address		Apt. #

City	State/Prov.	Zip/Postal Code

Signature (if under 18, a parent or guardian must sign)

Mail to the **Reader Service:**
IN U.S.A.: P.O. Box 1867, Buffalo, NY 14240-1867
IN CANADA: P.O. Box 609, Fort Erie, Ontario L2A 5X3

**Are you a current subscriber to Harlequin Presents® books
and want to receive the larger-print edition?
Call 1-800-873-8635 or visit www.ReaderService.com.**

* Terms and prices subject to change without notice. Prices do not include applicable taxes. Sales tax applicable in N.Y. Canadian residents will be charged applicable taxes. Offer not valid in Quebec. This offer is limited to one order per household. Not valid for current subscribers to Harlequin Presents books. All orders subject to credit approval. Credit or debit balances in a customer's account(s) may be offset by any other outstanding balance owed by or to the customer. Please allow 4 to 6 weeks for delivery. Offer available while quantities last.

Your Privacy—The Reader Service is committed to protecting your privacy. Our Privacy Policy is available online at www.ReaderService.com or upon request from the Reader Service.

We make a portion of our mailing list available to reputable third parties that offer products we believe may interest you. If you prefer that we not exchange your name with third parties, or if you wish to clarify or modify your communication preferences, please visit us at www.ReaderService.com/consumerschoice or write to us at Reader Service Preference Service, P.O. Box 9062, Buffalo, NY 14240-9062. Include your complete name and address.

HP15

SPECIAL EXCERPT FROM

HARLEQUIN

Presents.

*Harlequin Presents® is thrilled to welcome
reader-favorite **Anne Mather** back to the
series with this fantastic story of forbidden passion
and hidden secrets!*

*Irish tycoon Jack Connolly had sworn off women after
a tragic accident cost him his wife. Haunted by her
memory, it is only when he meets Grace Spencer that
his senses are awakened. But she is out of bounds for
she belongs to another...or does she?*

Read on for a sneak preview of
A FORBIDDEN TEMPTATION

"We—we have to go," she said, but her voice was thready
and barely audible.

Jack nodded. "Yeah," he said hoarsely, but then he
bent his head and covered her lips with his, and she fairly
melted against him.

Which was so wrong. But just at that moment it felt so
incredibly right.

Jack thought his body might go up in flames. The
yielding softness of her mouth beneath his was that
devastating.

Her lips were moist and sensuous, igniting a flame
inside him that was damn near irresistible. His hands slid
down her arms and linked with hers. And it was the most
natural thing in the world to wind her hands behind her
back and urge her even closer against him.

HPEXP0216

Grace, meanwhile, could feel her senses slipping. What little resistance she had left was drifting away. And when Jack's tongue parted her lips and thrust hungrily into her mouth, she couldn't prevent her nails from digging urgently into his palms.

But that was only part of it, he acknowledged grimly. What he really wanted he couldn't have. He blew out a breath.

That wasn't going to happen.

Not in this lifetime. No way.

And the sooner he put a stop to this, the sooner he'd remember who he was. Who *she* was.

He had to kill these feelings that were so—unwanted? Right.

With a determination that was enforced by the belief that Grace would blame him for this, Jack reluctantly released her hands and stepped away from her.

Not far, because the window was at his back. But far enough for her to realize what he was doing.

"Like you said," he declared, his voice a little rough. He cleared his throat before continuing, "We should go."

Don't miss
A FORBIDDEN TEMPTATION by Anne Mather,
available March 2016 wherever
Harlequin® Historical books and ebooks are sold.

www.Harlequin.com

Copyright © 2016 by Anne Mather

HPEXP0216